QUESTS FOR FIRE

QUESTS FOR FIRE

FOR

TALES FROM MANY LANDS

RETOLD BY
JON C. STOTT

ILLUSTRATIONS BY
THEO DOMBROWSKI

VICTORIA · VANCOUVER · CALGARY

Heritage House Publishing Company Ltd.
heritagehouse.ca

LIBRARY AND ARCHIVES CANADA CATALOGUING IN PUBLICATION

Stott, Jon C., 1939–
  Quest for fire: tales from many lands / [retold by] Jon C. Stott.

Includes bibliographical references. Issued also in electronic format.
ISBN 978-1-927051-59-7

  I. Title.

PZ8.1.S886Qu 2012   j398.26   C2012-902685-9

editor Grenfell Featherstone
proofreader Karla Decker
cover and interior designer Jacqui Thomas

MIX
Paper from
responsible sources
FSC® C103567

The interior of this book was produced using 100% post-consumer recycled paper, processed chlorine free and printed with vegetable-based inks.

Heritage House acknowledges the financial support for its publishing program from the Government of Canada through the Canada Book Fund (CBF), Canada Council for the Arts and the province of British Columbia through the British Columbia Arts Council and the Book Publishing Tax Credit.

Canadian Heritage
Patrimoine canadien

The Canada Council
for the Arts
Le Conseil des Arts
du Canada

BRITISH COLUMBIA
ARTS COUNCIL

16 15 14 13 12 1 2 3 4 5

Printed in Canada

CONTENTS

iNTRODUCTiON

Fire. Nowadays, this word often suggests sitting around a campfire on a summer evening, roasting hot dogs, telling stories and singing songs. For some people, fire may not have such happy associations. They may remember seeing blazing buildings or forests turned into infernos.

However, most modern people do not have much direct contact with fire. Electricity, natural gas and microwaves provide energy for cooking, light or warmth. That was not the case when the stories in this collection were first told. For most of human history, people depended on fire. Without it, they would be cold and wet; they would spend their nights in darkness and eat their food raw.

Because it was so important to them, people often told stories about fire: what their lives would be like without it, how they first acquired it and how possessing it changed their lives. The heroes of these stories are very different from each other. Some were well-known leaders and some were insignificant members of their groups. Some made their quests for fire alone and some worked with others. Some were brave and unselfish and some sought personal glory. The audiences of these stories, especially children, learned about good and bad behaviour. The stories of fire quests were so important that they were passed on from generation to generation.

Quests for Fire contains nine stories from different parts of the world. I hope they entertain you and help you better understand the lives of the people who first told them.

HOW OPOSSUM
BROUGHT FIRE BACK TO THE PEOPLE

guana had never gotten along very well with his wife and mother-in-law. After a major quarrel one night, Iguana became so angry that he waited until the two women had gone to sleep and then stole the fire that was burning outside all the huts in the rancho. He gathered it all together and began to climb the steep cliffs that were near the village.

He was very happy when he arrived at the top. He wouldn't have to live with his wife and mother-in-law anymore, and he knew that they would be miserable without the fire. They'd have to eat their food raw, and when the cold, dry weather set in, they wouldn't be able to keep warm. It didn't bother him that everyone else in the rancho would suffer as well. He'd never really liked any of them anyway.

Iguana was pretty sure that no one would be able to take the fire away from him. The path he'd taken up the cliff was too steep for the others to climb. Even if they made it some of the way, the great waterfall that thundered down from far above would block their path. And if any invaders made it to the top, they'd be exhausted and the air would be so thin that they would be gasping for breath.

He would build his house so that he could see the edges of the great flat-topped mountain in every direction. Even if invaders could overcome all the obstacles, he'd be able to see them coming and could hide the fire.

In the early-winter morning after Iguana had left the rancho, the people discovered their loss. They gathered in groups in front of their huts. Their breath formed clouds in the cold air, and although their brightly coloured shirts and blouses looked warm, everyone shivered.

"Where is the fire?" they asked each other. Then they noticed the tracks of Iguana leading off to the cliffs.

"He must be very angry," his wife said, and she told them about the quarrel. "He has taken all the fire into the sky."

"How are we going to get it back?" they asked each other.

They held meetings for five days. They had to stop their discussions each day when the sun went down, however, because they were cold. They had to go back to their homes to wrap themselves in *rebozos* to stay warm during the long night.

Near the end of the fifth day, Raven, who had always thought he was the brightest one in the rancho, announced that he would fly to the mountaintop. When he spotted Iguana's house, he would find a way to trick Iguana and steal back the fire. Everyone wished him well, and he circled the village before winging his way toward the cliffs.

It wasn't as easy as he thought it would be. He had no difficulty following the trail that Iguana had made. But as it went up and up and up, the air became thinner and thinner, and he had to perch on a ledge of the cliff, gasping for breath. He could see where the trail disappeared behind a waterfall that was so high, it seemed to come from the sky. He flew around and around, trying to find where the trail came out, but he discovered nothing. By now, the sun was low in the west. Cold, exhausted and hungry, Raven flew back to the rancho.

When he landed, the villagers clustered around him, eagerly asking him what he'd done with the fire.

"It is impossible for us to get the fire," said Raven. "It is too far, and the air is too thin. I am the best flyer in all the rancho and the cleverest of all. If I can't bring back the fire, no one can."

The people of the rancho were disappointed. But they were determined to reclaim their fire. To spend the rest of their lives eating their food raw and shivering in the cold would be too miserable. They would have another meeting the following day.

The next day, Hummingbird volunteered to go after the fire. "I can fly much higher than Raven, and when I get to the mesa, I'll be so small that Iguana will never be able to spot me." But the next evening, he returned to the rancho without fire.

For many days, the villagers held meetings. Each time someone would confidently proclaim that they would reclaim the fire, they would return in the evening without it.

One morning, when nearly everyone had given up hope, Opossum called the others together and told them that he would try. They were surprised to see him, because he usually slept all day. People shook their heads. They wondered how this fat, bushy-tailed, waddling member of the rancho would climb the steep trail along the cliff. And if he ever made it to the top, he moved so slowly that Iguana would spot him very quickly.

"Perhaps," Opossum replied. "But at least let me try. Now I need to get my sleep."

He waddled to his house and wasn't seen again until sunset. Then the villagers watched him move slowly along the trail that led to the cliffs.

Opossum climbed the cliff very carefully and slowly, using his long tail to help him keep his balance. He didn't want to slip, and he didn't want to start breathing too quickly in the thin air. When he reached the great waterfall, he looked around. He noticed that the trail disappeared behind the curtain of water. He moved cautiously forward, pressing his body against the rock wall so that the powerful waters wouldn't knock him off the cliff.

Opossum hadn't gone far when he saw that the trail didn't come out on the other side of the waterfall. Instead, it entered a tunnel in the cliff. *That's why the others didn't succeed*, he thought to himself. *They didn't know the trail went into a tunnel*. He walked into the darkness. The path began to slope steeply upward. He moved cautiously through the darkness for a very long time. Finally, he saw daylight in the distance.

Soon Opossum stood on the flat top of the mountain. He looked around for Iguana's home. In the distance, smoke rose into the blue sky. *That must be where Iguana took the fire,* he thought to himself. *I don't know how I'm going to get the fire, but if I'm careful, I may be able to get close to it and look around. Then maybe I can make a plan.*

Opossum was frightened because he knew he was

much smaller and slower than Iguana. He knew that Iguana could see things that were far away and that Iguana might spot him long before he got to the fire. He remembered Iguana's bad temper. He feared what would happen if he got caught.

Sure enough, Opossum had made it only a short way toward the smoke when Iguana saw him and rushed forward, shrieking, "What are you doing here, Opossum? Are you trying to steal my fire? There's no use trying to run away. I'm going to catch you, and then I'll find out how good roasted opossum tastes."

Opossum was terrified. His heart began to beat faster and faster, and then, just as Iguana reached him, Opossum collapsed.

The lizard stopped in amazement. *I think I've frightened Opossum to death,* he thought as he walked around the still body and poked it with a stick. *At least he's saved me the trouble of having to kill him.* He grabbed Opossum's long, woolly tail and dragged him over to where the fire was burning.

Leaving the body beside the fire, Iguana went inside his house. *I'm not that hungry right now,* he said to himself. *I'll have a nap before I start preparing my dinner.*

But Opossum wasn't dead. He had just fainted with fright. He came to shortly after Iguana had gone inside. He looked carefully around and could see the lizard's tracks leading to the house. Then he heard snoring.

I think that if I could get some fire, I could get back to the tunnel before he wakes up, thought Opossum. *But how am I going to get the fire?*

Opossum knew that he'd have to come up with a plan quickly. It was getting late in the afternoon, and Iguana would soon be awake and feeling very hungry. Opossum came up with one idea after another, but each of them had difficulties and dangers that made the possibility of success very small.

He'd just about given up and was considering sneaking back to the tunnel when he smelled something burning. A spark from the fire had landed on the fur of his tail and was smouldering. *That's it!* Opossum thought. *I won't have to carry a stick of fire. I'll be the carrier myself. That way I can use all four legs to get to the tunnel before Iguana wakes up.*

Opossum moved away from the fire and Iguana's house as quietly and quickly as he could. He could feel the ember burning into the skin of his tail, but he tried to ignore the pain. The important thing was to get away.

He'd nearly reached the entrance to the tunnel when he heard Iguana just behind him.

Again Opossum was filled with terror, and again he fainted. Iguana arrived and once again poked him with a stick. Then he sniffed the air. *It seems my friend has burned himself. I left him too close to the fire,* he thought. *He wouldn't be worth eating now. He'd taste too bad. I'm glad that he wasn't able to steal any of my fire.*

Iguana didn't notice the ember that was nestled in the fur near the base of Opossum's tail.

Iguana grabbed Opossum by the tail. But this time, instead of dragging him back to his home, he dragged him to the tunnel opening and dropped him inside.

I don't think anyone at the rancho will discover the

tunnel behind the waterfall, he thought. *But just in case, I'll make sure that nobody is able to come through it onto the mesa.* Then he pushed several very large stones into the opening.

Inside the tunnel, the spark glowed red and burned the fur all the way to the skin on Opossum's tail. The pain woke him up. *I'm still alive, and I've still got the fire with me! But I'd better get back to the rancho as quickly as I can or I'll be burned to death.* He moved through the tunnel until he came to the waterfall.

What now? Opossum wondered. *I'd sure like to put the fire out and cool my body in the waterfall. But then I'd have failed at my job.*

He looked over his shoulder at his tail. The fur was burned off half of it, but the part near the tip was still smoking. He tucked his tail between his hind legs and edged his way along the trail between the cliff and the waterfall. The mist and spray dampened the fur on his back. The ember burned his stomach, but at least it didn't go out.

When Opossum came out from behind the waterfall, he lifted his tail in the air. His body and tail hurt dreadfully where they had been burned. The beautiful fluffy hair on his tail was nearly gone. He was worried because he had a long way to go to get to the rancho, and it looked like there wasn't enough hair left to keep the fire burning.

There was only one thing Opossum could do. Carefully he curved his tail so that the ember touched his back. The fur didn't catch fire right away because it was still damp from the waterfall. But soon he smelled smoke.

The wet fur didn't burn quickly. But Opossum still had

a long way to go before he reached the village. By the time he arrived at the rancho, nearly all of the hair from his back had been burned off.

At first the villagers didn't recognize him. "Who's that stranger?" they called to each other. "Let's chase him away." And they picked up sticks and started running toward Opossum.

"Stop!" he shouted. "It's me. And I've brought the fire back."

The villagers were amazed when they saw who it was. But where was the fire?

"Quickly!" he said. "Get some dry straw and some small twigs. Don't ask questions, or it will be too late!"

He told the villagers to hold some straw next to the spot where the ember was still burning. Soon little flames burst from the ends of the pieces of straw. "Hold the flames against the twigs until they catch fire," Opossum ordered.

Soon the people had a small fire burning. "Don't let it run out of wood," Opossum told them. Then he walked over to the stream at the edge of the rancho and stepped into the very cold water to soothe his burned body. When he crawled out of the water and rolled in the sand, the burned hair fell off his tail and body.

It was a very different-looking Opossum who came back into the village and stood by the fire to warm himself. His body had almost no hair on it, and his tail was completely bare. But the villagers didn't laugh. "You do look different, Opossum," one of them said to him. "But when we see how you look now, we will remember how brave you were, and how you suffered great danger and pain to help us all."

And to this day, when the Cora people of central Mexico see an opossum, they remember the story of his courage, and they do not laugh at how odd he looks.

And to this day, all opossums faint when danger threatens them. They know that their enemies will think they are dead and will walk away without hurting them.

WHY THE SELFISH WATERRATS SHARE FIRE

:: **Many traditional Australian tales about the origins of fire were set in a time when different types of animals lived together. The various characters in these stories interact in ways that reveal good and bad behaviour.**

R akali, the waterrat, and his wife, Nibulin, didn't particularly like the other villagers. They seldom joined in community activities, and they wouldn't stop to talk to others they passed along the trail.

"I think," Rakali said to his wife, "that we should find somewhere else to live, somewhere where there aren't so many people, and where there's water close by so that I don't have to travel so far when I bring home the fish I catch."

Nibulin thought that was a wonderful idea and encouraged Rakali to start looking for a place right away.

It didn't take very long. Late the next afternoon, he returned home with a smile on his face. "I've found the perfect place," he told Nibulin. "It's right next to a billabong. The water's not too deep, and there are plenty of fish. There are some coolabah trees to give us shade on hot summer days. And there's a little meadow where we can put our fish out to dry in the sun. Come and take a look."

When Nibulin saw the billabong, she was delighted. She pointed to a spot on the bank and said, "Why don't you start digging? We'll make a small burrow right now and later we can make it bigger. I'll head back to our place and start packing. I can't wait to get out of that village."

The ground was very soft, and soon Rakali had made a snug little room. He returned to his wife just as the sun was setting. Nibulin had packed everything and was sitting impatiently at the door. She wanted to go to the billabong right away. But when her husband told her that it would soon be too dark to see their way, she agreed to wait until the morning.

The two left the village just as the sky began to turn grey. They carried the few things they owned in sacks slung over their shoulders. Nobody else was stirring yet, which didn't bother them. There really wasn't anyone to whom they wanted to say goodbye.

Over the next few days, they worked busily getting their new home set up. Each day, Rakali would fish in the morning and lay out his catch to dry on a stump in the meadow. Then he would help Nibulin dig under the ground to make their home bigger. In the evenings, while they ate the dried fish Rakali had caught, they would discuss how happy they were in their new home.

One night, they heard a great *caribberie* in the village. As the festive sounds reached them, Rakali turned to his wife and remarked, "I'd rather be here than at that festival—too much noise and too many people."

The next afternoon, Rakali emerged from his tunnel much earlier than usual. He was pressing one of his paws against his jaw. When his wife asked what the matter was, he explained: "I was digging when I came to a big root from one of the coolabah trees. I tried to pull it, but it wouldn't budge, so I decided to gnaw at it. My teeth slipped and hit a rock. My mouth really hurts."

The next day, the same thing happened, but with one difference. Rakali noticed that when his tooth glanced against the rock, a little bit of light seemed to jump from the rock and land on him. Before the spark died, he noticed that his fur smelled funny and that his skin hurt where the light had landed. He told his wife what had happened.

"I'm going to join you tomorrow afternoon," she said. "I want to see this."

When Nibulin saw the spark the next day, she told her husband, "I'm going to try to make a light myself." She bit into the rock and saw the speck of light glow for a moment when it landed on her. She felt the burning on her skin and smelled her singed hair.

Several days later, on a warm autumn evening, Nibulin looked toward the western horizon and remarked, "The sun is certainly setting much earlier. In a few weeks, it will be pretty cold, and we won't be sitting out here having our evening meal."

Then she sat for a long time, looking at the setting sun and saying nothing. As the red ball of flame met the edge of the land, she again spoke. "I've been thinking about those sparks that came off the rock. They were bright, and they were hot. If we could find a way to get more of them without hurting our teeth and learn to keep them from going out so quickly, we wouldn't be so cold and damp when winter comes. We'd also have light so that we could see better at night."

The next afternoon, Nibulin watched carefully as Rakali began digging in the tunnel. Suddenly he said, "Ouch!" and backed up. He was holding one front paw with the other.

"What's the matter?" she asked, a worried note in her voice. "What have you done to your hand?"

He held his paw toward her. There was a very small trickle of blood on it.

"You've cut yourself, but not very badly. Let's see if we can find what hurt you." Together, they dug carefully in the mud.

"Here's something," Rakali said. He showed her a small, sharp-edged stone in the mud.

That evening, as the two watched the setting sun after dinner, Nibulin exclaimed, "Ah, ha! I've thought of something! That rock you stepped on was pretty hard, at least as hard as your teeth. Maybe if we took it and banged it against another rock, we'd get a spark. If we hit it hard enough, we might get a lot of sparks."

And so, the next afternoon, Rakali and Nibulin searched for rocks in the tunnel. They soon found a small sharp rock like the one that had cut Rakali the day before. Soon after, they found a large, rough rock that was sticking out of the muddy walls of the tunnel. Rakali struck the small rock against the big one and a shower of sparks leapt out and fell downward. But all of the sparks went out before they hit the muddy ground.

Excited, he struck the rock again. More sparks. He began hitting the rock again and again, faster and faster. Suddenly he stopped. He dropped the small rock and cried out in pain. Some of the sparks had landed on the fur on his arm. A very small flame rose from the fur and then went out.

"That's enough for today," Nibulin said soothingly. "We don't want you to get hurt anymore. But now I know how to trap the sparks and keep them alive. Tomorrow I'll show you." She found the sharp stone that Rakali had dropped and, clutching it in her paw, she walked upward out of the tunnel and into the daylight.

The next afternoon, when Rakali headed toward the tunnel, Nibulin told him to stop. "We have to go out to the clearing first."

Puzzled, he followed her. In the field, she pulled up three or four clumps of dried grass, handed them to him and walked back to the tunnel, stopping first to pick up the sharp stone.

When they reached the spot where the larger rock stuck out, she took the grass from him and told him to begin striking with the sharp rock. "But strike downwards so that the sparks won't get in your fur." She held the clump of grass just below where he would strike.

The sparks began to fly as he brought the sharp stone down on the big rock. Some of them hit the grass and started little flames. But they quickly went out. One of the flying sparks fell on her paw. She drew her paw back quickly and, as she did, the straw flamed more brightly.

But not for long.

"When I pulled my paw back," she remarked to Rakali, "I felt a tiny breeze. That's when the flame on the straw got bigger. Maybe I should blow gently on the sparks when they land." She did, and pretty soon the clump of grass burned with a large flame. But her paw started to get very hot, and she dropped the burning straw onto the mud floor, where it went out.

"That's enough for today, Rakali. Let's have our fish and think about this some more."

The next day, along with clumps of grass, the waterrats

picked up some twigs. Back in the tunnel, Nibulin told Rakali to put some of the grass on the floor and lean a few of the twigs against it. She held some straw near the rock. He hit it, and the sparks flew. She blew on the red glow in the straw, and, when it burst into flames, he leaned over and touched the flame to the straw on the ground. It caught on fire, and soon the flame spread to the sticks.

After the little blaze had died down, Nibulin smiled. "Now we know how to capture the sparks. Tomorrow we'll bring a big stick and lots of twigs and straw into the tunnel. When we get the big stick burning, we can bring it up and start a fire near the entry to our home."

And that's how Rakali and Nibulin discovered how to make fire.

As the days grew shorter and the nights longer, the burning sticks at the front of their home gave them light and warmth.

One day, after Rakali had caught fish, Nibulin decided to hold them close to the fire. "There isn't very much warmth in the sun now, and it takes so long for the fish to dry, maybe the fire would do a quicker job." And so she discovered the secret of cooking.

Rakali and Nibulin were very content. They were warm and dry and had light after the sun set. Not only that, but the fish they ate tasted much better cooked than dried.

"Think of all the poor people back in the village—cold and damp and eating dried fish in the darkness," Nibulin remarked. She really wasn't sorry for them. She had never liked them. If they were feeling miserable, that made her feel good. "I'm never going to let them know our secret about fire. If they ever found out that we had fire and asked for some, I'd tell them to quit bothering us."

It would have upset both Rakali and Nibulin if they had known that nobody in the village missed them. In fact, nobody even talked about them.

Not until one morning.

In the pale light of early dawn, Owl returned to the village after his night of hunting and exploring. He called to the other villagers, "Wake up, everyone. I have something very important to tell you."

The villagers came out of their homes, rubbing their eyes. "What happened to you?" one of them asked. "Your feathers are all smudged. We will call you Sooty Owl."

Sooty Owl turned his head in a complete circle, looking at his back and wings. "So they are. I think it has something to do with what I want to tell you. Last night I was flying over the river, and by the billabong where the waterrats went to live, I saw a yellow-and-red light. I flew closer and saw Rakali and Nibulin sitting together outside their burrow. In front of them was a pile of glowing sticks, with some fish propped up near it. The fish smelled delicious.

"Rakali gave Nibulin a hug and said to her, 'Isn't this fire wonderful? We are so warm in the cold evenings, and fish tastes so much better when it's cooked instead of just dried. It's our own wonderful secret. I'll never share it with anyone else.'

"I took another circle around the billabong, gliding so low that I passed through the smoke that was coming up from the flames. That must be how I got so dirty. The two waterrats certainly looked warm."

All the animals were very excited about what Sooty Owl had told them. They wanted what the waterrats had. They wanted warmth and light and delicious food. After much discussion, they decided they would visit the billabong later that afternoon and try to get some fire from Rakali and Nibulin.

As the sun began its slow journey to the western horizon, the group started toward the billabong, chattering noisily among themselves. When they came to the cleared ground outside the waterrats' home, they could see no fire, just a pile of dirt and mud with some smoke rising from it.

Rakali and Nibulin had heard them coming and quickly extinguished the flames.

Lizard spoke for the group. "Rakali and Nibulin, you know that the people of the village share things with each other. We have come to ask you to share this fire with us."

Nibulin looked at Lizard and the others as if they weren't worthy of being in her company. Then she replied very condescendingly, "That is what you may do in the village. But you seem to forget that we do not live in the village. We don't have to share anything with you, and we won't." She turned away from the group and began talking to Rakali as if the villagers weren't even there.

When the animals returned to the village, they were very angry. What should they do now? That fire would really be wonderful to have during the long cold nights that lay ahead.

"We'll have to steal it," they said. "We'll send the quietest person in the village to the billabong tonight to sneak up and grab one of the burning sticks." They all agreed that wise old Turtle should be the one to go.

Turtle moved very quietly so that the waterrats didn't hear him. But they did see him when he came into the clearing near their home. He was walking so slowly that Rakali and Nibulin had plenty of time to grab the burning sticks and throw them into the billabong.

"You'll have to move faster than that," Rakali laughed unkindly before he and Nibulin turned their backs and went into their burrow.

The villagers then decided that they needed someone fast and fierce, someone who could get to the fire sticks before the waterrats extinguished them and who could frighten them if they hid the fire. Everyone agreed that Kangaroo would be the best choice.

Kangaroo could certainly hop over a lot of ground in a short time, but he wasn't at all quiet. The waterrats heard him coming, and of course the fire was gone by the time he arrived. They hid in their home, which was far too small for Kangaroo to get into, so he stood at the doorway shaking his fists and threatening them.

But they just laughed. "You're a bigger failure than Turtle," they sneered.

When they met again, the villagers realized that they had run out of solutions. "We must ask Eaglehawk," someone ventured. "He is very fierce and very proud, but he is also very wise. If we show him how much respect we have for him, he may help."

They went to the red gum tree by the big river and called up to Eaglehawk. He was perched high above the ground at the edge of his nest. He flew to a lower branch, and, after he heard their problem, he said he would help. Although he and his family lived alone, he said that he agreed with the villagers' custom of sharing, and he thought that the water-rats were behaving very badly.

Later that afternoon, Eaglehawk flew so high into the sky that he was only a speck. Then the villagers couldn't see him at all. But he could see them. His eyes were so sharp that he could clearly see the land far below.

He spotted Rakali heading home at the end of the day.

Eaglehawk dove from high in the sky to the ground, as fast as lightning travels from a cloud to a tall tree in the forest. Before Rakali had reached the middle of the clearing, the great bird had grabbed him in his claws.

Rakali was terrified. "Don't feed me to your family, please," he whimpered.

"I don't want to eat you," Eaglehawk replied. "I want you to tell me how you get fire. And I want you to tell me very quickly. We're getting pretty high in the air, and if I don't learn your secret very quickly, I'll let go of you. You'll hit the ground right in front of your house, and you won't need any more fires after that."

Rakali quickly agreed. He really did love his wife, and he wanted to share many, many evenings with her in front of the fire. So he promised to show Eaglehawk how to make fire.

They landed just in front of the waterrats' home. His wife was hiding inside.

"Come out right now, Nibulin," Rakali commanded. Even though he was very frightened, he tried to sound as if he were in control of the situation. He hoped that Eaglehawk wouldn't notice the fear in his voice.

He told Nibulin to bring handfuls of dried grass from the clearing. Then, when she'd done that, he sent her into the brush to gather dried twigs. Finally, he ordered her to bring the fire-making stones from inside.

Rakali's paws trembled so badly that he had to try many times before he was able to hit the rocks and make sparks to light the straw. When the fire was burning brightly, he said to Eaglehawk, "That is how you do it. It's really a very simple little secret. It's very easy." Then he handed Nibulin the two stones and said, "You'd better take these back into the house."

"Not so fast," Eaglehawk said. He quickly placed himself between Nibulin and the house. "I'll take the stones with me. You'll have to find some new ones for yourself."

Rakali was about to argue. But after he had looked at the bird's fierce talons and cruel mouth and seen the angry glint in his eye, he decided to say nothing.

The two waterrats watched the great bird fly toward the village with a fire stone clasped in each claw. Then they sat down to eat a dinner of raw fish. The night was very cold, and they huddled in each other's arms to keep warm.

It took them several days of digging in the dark tunnels before they found two more stones that would make sparks. Once they did, they were able to cook their fish and stay warm.

To this day, waterrats have no desire to live with the other animals. It's not that they still think they're too good for other people; it is that they are ashamed of how they behaved.

WHY THE PEOPLE RESPECT
TORTOISE AND CHAMELEON

BENIN

:: There are two main seasons in West Africa: dry and rainy. Although the rainy season is essential to support life, people can become miserable during the great rainstorms because they get wet and cold when they go outside, and their homes are dark and damp inside. People depend on fire to keep them warm and dry and to supply light. This story from the country of Benin explains not only how the people got fire, but also how they were tested by the creator, Mawu.

When the rainy season came, the people really wanted fire. Sometimes it would pour for days. The clouds made the sky so dark that they could hardly see to work in their huts. Everything was damp. When windstorms joined the rain, the people would get drenched whenever they had to go outside.

It wasn't that there wasn't any fire. Mawu, the creator of the world, had made fire. However, she wouldn't share it with the sky people or the earth people. Instead, she placed it in the land between the sky and the earth and then commanded Agbakankan to guard it very carefully. No one knew why Mawu was so protective of the fire.

At first, Agbakankan guarded the fire very carefully. Whenever he saw something move in the distance, he grabbed his sharply pointed spears, shook them in the air and called out savagely that if anyone was out there, that person had better go away very quickly.

After a while, Agbakankan began to get bored with watching the fire. When the rains started, people stayed in their huts most of the time, so he couldn't even enjoy shaking his spears and yelling out savagely anymore. He was warm and dry, sitting at the entrance of his small hut, gazing at the fire, but the days seemed to drag by.

Sometimes the heat from the fire would make him drowsy, and he wished that he could take an afternoon nap. So he caught two chachue birds, the only other creatures Mawu allowed near fire, to keep watch for him. He trained them to look into the distance for any movement and to shriek if they saw anyone approaching. Now that he had two lookouts, Agbakankan could take long afternoon naps whenever he wished.

Back in the village, the people decided to have a meeting. None of the huts was big enough to hold them all, so they stood in the rain, which seemed to be coming down harder than anyone could remember. The wind whipped the rain against them. They were cold and miserable. They had to do something.

"Mawu gave us language so we could talk together," someone said.

"And she gave us intelligence," another replied.

"There must be some reason she made fire and decided that we couldn't have it," remarked a third person.

"Perhaps," said a voice that came from very close to the ground, "there is a reason for all of these things." It was Tortoise. He didn't speak very often, and he spoke softly. So when he did speak, everyone listened very carefully. "Mawu wouldn't have given us language or intelligence if she didn't want us to use them. Maybe she wants us to work together to find a way to get fire," Tortoise continued.

Immediately, all of the people started to talk. Everyone

had an idea. Nobody listened to anyone else. Suddenly, Lion stood up, shook his mane and roared loudly. Everyone stopped talking and looked at him.

"I am the strongest and bravest of everyone," he said proudly. "I will go to get Mawu's fire. When Agbakankan and his two chachue birds see me, they will be so terrified that they won't be able to do anything. I'll walk up to the fire, take some of it and bring it back."

Even though the rain had plastered his usually magnificent mane against his neck, Lion walked proudly out of the village. He trotted for a long time across the savannah until he saw the glow of fire in the distance. Had he been hunting for his dinner, he would have crouched low and slunk slowly and quietly through the grass until he was close enough to rush at his prey. But today Lion kept walking proudly forward. If anyone were watching the fire, they would certainly be afraid of him and run away.

The chachue birds were so busy roasting some food that they didn't notice Lion until he let out his loudest and fiercest roar. They had never heard anything like it, and they'd never seen anything as big and fierce as Lion. They were so frightened that they could only make feeble squeaks instead of their warning cries.

Lion walked up to the fire, picked up two embers, wrapped them in wet grass and put them carefully into his mouth. If he'd used the intelligence Mawu had given him, he would have run quickly away. Instead, he walked slowly and regally from the fire.

The chachue birds recovered their voices. They began to shriek loudly. Agbakankan had been enjoying his long afternoon nap. He awoke with a start and stumbled to the door of the hut, rubbing his eyes.

"What is happening?" he asked.

"Lion has stolen the fire," the birds cried out together, and they pointed onto the savannah, where the thief was strolling away, head still held high.

Agbakankan feared what Mawu might do if she learned that he'd failed his duties. He rushed into his hut, grabbed two of his sharpest spears and came out running and yelling.

Lion looked over his shoulder. *I'll just let out one of my most frightening roars*, he thought to himself. *That will scare Agbakankan so much that I'll be able to get away easily.*

And so he opened his mouth, dropped the coals onto the ground and roared. Agbakankan kept coming. He was more frightened of Mawu's anger than of anything Lion might do. Lion roared again. But his pursuer kept coming closer.

Agbakankan stopped, pulled one arm back and hurled a spear with all his strength. It hit Lion on one of his back legs. Then another spear flew through the air and hit the other back leg. Lion opened his mouth and roared again. But this time, it was a roar of pain. He rolled over on the muddy ground, knocking the spears loose, and then ran back to the village as fast as he could. In his haste, he forgot to pick up the smouldering coals. Agbakankan gathered them up and returned them to the fire at his hut.

When Lion arrived at the village, the people crowded around, asking, "Where is the fire?"

"I couldn't get it," he responded. "I tried many times to

get close, but Agbakankan always found a way to keep the fire away from me. He is very, very clever."

Most of the villagers looked disappointed. Lion had been so confident when he left the village, they'd been sure they would soon have fire to make them warm and dry.

As Lion told his story, one of the villagers had to work very hard to hide a smile. It was Elephant. Whenever Lion boasted about how important he was, Elephant would feel angry and jealous. He wanted to be the most important and respected one in the village. After all, he was much bigger than Lion, and he could make a trumpeting noise that was every bit as loud as his rival's roar.

When the villagers had their next meeting, Elephant trumpeted loudly, silencing everyone else. "I will go to take the fire from Agbakankan. Soon you will all be warm and dry." And before anyone could say anything, he turned and walked proudly out of the village, waving his great ears back and forth and holding his trunk high in the air.

When Elephant came close to the chachue birds, he trumpeted loudly. *That will scare them*, he thought. But it didn't.

So he charged. His huge feet sent mud splattering up on his legs and body, but the chachue birds just stood and watched him.

He skidded to a stop at the edge of a very deep trench that circled around the place where the fire glowed. Large, sharp spikes pointed up from the bottom of the pit. Evidently, Agbakankan hadn't spent all his time napping after he had chased Lion away. He wasn't going to take a chance that another villager would get close to the fire.

The birds didn't give any screeching warnings, and Agbakankan didn't rush out of his hut with spears in each hand. It wasn't necessary. There was no way Elephant would be able to get across the deep pit. He trudged back home.

The people were waiting expectantly, sure that Elephant would bring the fire to them. But before they could ask where it was, Elephant spoke. "Lion was right. Agbakankan is very clever. It was impossible for me to get the fire from him."

The people sat in gloomy silence—all except Tortoise and Chameleon, who stood at the edge of the group talking very quietly to each other.

"I have an idea," Tortoise finally said to the unhappy group. They looked at him, but without much interest. If Lion and Elephant had not succeeded, Tortoise certainly wouldn't have a chance.

Tortoise outlined his plan. "Instead of taking Mawu's fire, we must make our own. To do that, we will need straw and some small pieces of very dry wood. If we take straw and wood to the place where Agbakankan guards the fire, we can use the straw to make flames to set our own wood on fire."

"But where will we get dry wood and straw? Everything has been soaked by the rain." The villagers were very discouraged.

Tortoise instructed them. "If you look carefully, you will find some dead branches low on the trees. If you skin the bark and shave away some of the outside wood, the inside will be dry. Getting the straw will be much more difficult. Gede, the Lord of the Earth, has a supply of dry straw in his hut. But there is a man with a flute who plays a tune to warn him if someone comes near. Gede has strong spirit powers, and he is very dangerous. If anyone is caught trying to steal his straw, we will never see that person again."

This time, neither Lion nor Elephant volunteered to help. It sounded too dangerous. None of the other villagers stepped forward either.

"I was afraid that none of you would offer to make the trip," Tortoise continued. "So, before I spoke to you, I explained my plan to Chameleon. He will try to get the straw."

The people looked at the little reptile, whom they generally ignored. He looked so much like the brown muddy ground that they could hardly see him. They didn't think he had much chance of coming back at all, let alone of coming back with the dry straw.

Unless he was scampering up a tree, Chameleon moved slowly. It took him three days to get to the place where Gede stored the dry straw. He watched the flute player and waited for his skin to take on the colour of the ground that lay between him and the straw. Then he moved forward so slowly that even if the flute player looked carefully, all he would see was a bump in the muddy ground.

Chameleon reached the straw and scurried under the pile of skins that protected it from the rain. Then he waited, listening carefully. When he heard the flute player sit down and begin to eat something, he carefully gathered a handful of the dry straw and edged himself out from under the skins. He waited for his skin to resume the colour of the muddy ground. Then he began moving away, holding the straw high in one hand.

The flute player finished his meal, stood up, stretched and

then turned in a circle, looking carefully in every direction. Of course, he couldn't see Chameleon, but much to his surprise, he saw a small bundle of straw disappear behind a baobab tree. *Something must be wrong,* he thought to himself and quickly began to play his flute.

Gede arrived and asked what the trouble was.

"I just saw a bunch of straw disappear behind that baobab tree. Maybe someone was stealing it," the flute player explained.

Gede rushed to the tree, circled around it and looked up into the branches. *There's nothing there*, he thought to himself, feeling just a little annoyed. *That foolish guard's eyes are playing tricks on him.* If Gede had looked more carefully, he would have noticed, high on the trunk, a lump that had the shape of a chameleon.

When Gede went away, Chameleon crept down the far side of the baobab and headed toward a mahogany tree in the distance. Just before he reached the other tree, the flute player once again saw the straw moving. He blinked his eyes to make sure he wasn't imagining things again. Then the straw disappeared behind the tree.

Once more he played his flute loudly. Once more Gede arrived. Once more he circled a tree, looked up in the branches and saw nothing, not even a lizard-shaped bump on the trunk. Once more he was angry with the guard. "Don't bother me again when you think you see some straw moving by itself."

And so, a few minutes later, when the guard saw a bundle of straw move away from the mahogany tree, he didn't reach for his flute. He just rubbed his eyes and scratched his head.

Because it was slower for him to walk when he was holding the straw, it took Chameleon four days to get home. The people didn't rush to greet him because they didn't want to hear about another failure. It was only when Chameleon called out, "Where's Tortoise? Tell him I have the straw!" that they decided to come out of their houses.

Chameleon didn't say anything to them but went to his own hut and waited for Tortoise to arrive. The villagers could hear them whispering to each other, but they couldn't make out what the two were saying.

After a while, Tortoise called out, "Bring four of the smallest, hardest and driest pieces of wood to my hut. Put them inside the door and then leave." The people did as they were told.

The next morning, just as darkness began to disappear, Tortoise walked slowly away from the village. The few people who had been outside and seen him depart were puzzled. "I didn't see him carrying any straw or wood," one said to the other. "He'll need those if he's ever going to bring fire home—which I doubt."

It took Tortoise five days to reach the place where the chachue birds kept watch over the fire. When they saw Tortoise, one of them said, "He's the slowest creature there is. Even if he gets some fire, he won't be able to escape. We don't need to wake Agbakankan." And they stopped watching him.

Tortoise moved closer and closer to the fire. When he was right beside it, he reached into a space under his shell and pulled out some straw and one of the sticks. He placed the straw on the fire. A wisp of smoke drifted upward, and then a small flame began to flicker. Tortoise held the stick over the flame. When the stick started to glow red, he placed it under his shell and began to walk away.

The two birds saw what he had done. They began to shriek, "Tortoise has stolen Mawu's fire. He is taking it back to the people."

Agbakankan woke up and rushed out of the hut. It didn't take him long to catch up with Tortoise, but he couldn't see any fire. To make sure, he turned Tortoise on his back. When he found nothing, he put him on his feet, apologized for treating him so roughly and then returned to the birds. "Don't bother me again, you foolish chachues. Tortoise didn't take anything." Agbakankan returned to his hut, lay down and went back to sleep.

It took Tortoise six days to get home. The first night, before he fell asleep under a baobab tree, he pulled the stick out of his shell. It had burned down to a very small piece. He reached into his shell again, pulled out a small handful of straw and another stick. He placed the straw on the ember, and when it began to flame he lit the second stick.

He did the same thing every evening. When he finally arrived at the village, he called out to the villagers as loudly as he could, "Quickly, quickly. Bring me some of the straw from my hut and some dry sticks."

Soon, four or five sticks were burning. The villagers were very happy as they looked at the flames.

"We can't just stand here looking at the fire," Tortoise told the villagers. "We need as much wood as we can get to keep the flames going. We'll start with dry pieces, and then, when there are a lot of flames, we can put on the wetter pieces. And if we stack more wet wood around the fire, we can dry it out."

Then he told everyone to build a small shelter by the doors to their huts. "You can keep a small fire burning there, and it won't go out when it rains."

That night it didn't rain. The people gathered around a large fire that was burning brightly in the centre of the village. They were warm, dry and happy. They were very proud of what Tortoise and Chameleon had done. "We are sorry that we didn't treat you with respect. You have done more for us than Lion and Elephant ever did."

Far away, while the villagers celebrated their fire, Mawu made surprise visits to Agbakankan and Gede. "You didn't do a very good job of keeping watch," she told them. "But I am not going to punish you. I really wanted the people to have fire, you see, but I wanted to make sure that they were worthy of it. Tortoise and Chameleon showed me that they were."

HOW COYOTE
AND HIS FRIENDS CAUGHT FIRE

UNiTED STATES :: The Karuk, who lived along the Klamath River in northern California, called themselves the Araar, the people. This fire story, about animals living and working together, reflects the Karuks' belief in democratic interrelationships and co-operation.

Shortly after the Araar had celebrated the salmon run and the acorn festival, the weather changed. The warm days of autumn turned into the cold, grey and damp days of early winter. Everyone suffered during the winter. But the bad weather was particularly hard on the very young, the very old and the sick, many of whom did not survive winter.

"If only we had fire," people would lament. "We would be warm and dry. We could see at night. And we could cook our dried salmon and make warm soup with the acorn powder."

The Araar had heard that there was fire in the world. They had heard that high on a distant mountain three very fierce Skookum women lived in a small house that had fire burning in a stone-lined pit. Although they were very old, the women had great spirit powers that they used to protect their fire. Stories were told about people who, long ago, had gone to beg for or to steal fire from the Skookum women. None had ever returned to the village.

After several days of fog and rain and cold nights, the villagers called a council. All of the adults crowded into the largest house. Everyone listened carefully to all the plans about how to get fire. They came up with many good ideas. However, after they had discussed each one carefully, they realized that they could not find a successful and safe way to get fire from the Skookums.

"We must find Coyote and ask for his help. He is certainly wiser than anyone else," they said.

Coyote didn't live in the village. He wandered around alone. Winter had never been a problem for him because his coat was very warm. When the people found him and told him about the suffering in the village, he agreed to come to their meeting the next day.

During the meeting, Coyote listened very carefully as the Araar told him about their suffering, about fire and about the Skookums. After they had finished, he sat quietly, thinking. Finally, he spoke. "I have a plan. It will be dangerous, but I think it will work. If we want fire, I will have to steal it from the Skookums. I will need five helpers." All of the animals volunteered. They wanted to help their people, and although they wouldn't admit it, some of them wanted to become heroes.

"I will need these people to help me," Coyote told the people. "Eagle, Mountain Lion, Squirrel, Chipmunk and Frog." Looks of surprise appeared on many faces. They could understand why Coyote had chosen Eagle and Mountain Lion—both were strong, brave and fierce. But Squirrel, Chipmunk and Frog?

"The rest of you must leave us alone now," Coyote said to the villagers. "We have a great deal of planning to do, and we will need quiet."

The six talked all night. At dawn, much to the villagers' surprise, the group didn't head for the forest path that led toward the mountain where the Skookums lived. Instead, they walked to the pond.

When the six reached the bank, Frog hopped away from them and sat at the edge of the water. The other five headed across the clearing toward the trail, and when they reached the heavy brush at the edge of the forest, Chipmunk left the group and sat under a low bush. The puzzled villagers wondered why Coyote had chosen Frog and Chipmunk and then left them behind.

They would have been more puzzled had they followed the others into the forest. After the brush thinned out, Squirrel hopped away, scurried up a tree and perched on a limb. When Coyote, Eagle and Mountain Lion reached the treeline, and nothing but scrub brush stretched upward toward the mountain peak where the Skookums lived, Mountain Lion stayed in the woods.

As Coyote and Eagle travelled up the slope, the rain that had been falling all day turned to sleet. The wind began to blow fiercely, and as they moved higher and higher, it became colder and colder.

When they had travelled nearly halfway up the steep slope, Eagle, who was flying above Coyote, called out, "I can see a thin wisp of smoke near the top of the mountain. It must be coming from the Skookums' house. I will leave you now." He soared higher and higher, disappearing into the snow clouds.

After Eagle had departed, Coyote rolled over and over on a patch of wet ground. He stood up and shook himself. His beautiful glossy coat had become muddy and matted. Shortly after the now-bedraggled Coyote started walking again, the sleet turned into snow. The wind whipped the wet flakes through the air, and Coyote couldn't see more than a few paces in front of him. *If I can't see up ahead, it means that the Skookums won't be able to see me,* he thought to himself.

Soon Coyote began to shiver. When it had snowed before, he had been in the forest and had kept dry and warm by curling up under low cedar branches. *Now I know how the others feel. It really is important for me to get the fire from the Skookums.*

"What's that out there?" A harsh, rasping voice came out of the blowing snow in front of Coyote. It was one of the Skookums. Coyote whined and whimpered. Then, cowering like a dog that expects to be hit, he moved slowly toward the voice.

"Did you find anything?" called someone from the house.

"Just a wet and dirty coyote," replied the harsh, rasping voice. "It's shivering and cold. I'll bring it in and let it warm itself beside the fire."

"You do look dreadful," she said to Coyote in a voice that didn't sound quite so harsh. "Come inside. We may even find some meat for you."

When Coyote came into the house, the first thing he noticed was the fire. It radiated a yellow-and-red glow as it crackled softly. He stepped toward the firepit, sniffing at the air. The smoke that rose to the hole in the roof left a sweet aroma in the air. He sat down beside the fire. The heat felt wonderful. He could see steam starting to rise from his wet, matted fur. He lay down, still shivering occasionally. The Skookum who had found him tossed him a piece of deer meat. He was hungry, and he ate it very quickly.

Coyote stretched out beside the fire, closed his eyes and

gave a deep sigh as if he were about to fall asleep. He was thinking that although getting into the house hadn't been that difficult, getting out with some fire would be very difficult. He would have to make sure that the Skookums were sleeping soundly. Then he could grab the end of one of the sticks that was burning in the fire and run.

It seemed as if the Skookums would never go to bed. They busied themselves with their evening chores, and then they sat talking. At last the three old spirit-women decided to go to sleep. The one who had brought Coyote inside turned to the youngest woman and said in the bossy way of older sisters, "The wood is running low. Bring an armful inside and put a couple of more logs on the fire before you go to sleep. It's going to get very cold tonight."

Grumbling, the younger one did as she was told and then lay down beside the other two. The flames rose up and the house became much warmer. By now, Coyote's fur had dried out, and he could feel himself becoming hotter and hotter. He would have liked to move a little way from the flames. But he knew that if he stirred, the Skookums would wake up and he wouldn't be able to carry out his plan.

He waited and waited, getting hotter and hotter. A spark jumped from the fire and landed on the long fluffy tail of which he was so proud. He could smell it smouldering in the fur. But he didn't dare move.

Although his tail started to smoke, and he was afraid that he would have to rush outside before it burst into flames, he still didn't move. Finally, he heard a faint snore and then another and another. The snores became louder. The three sisters were sound asleep. Coyote knew it was time to act.

Slowly, Coyote stood up. His muscles ached as he stretched. He bent his head over the edge of the firepit. One of the sticks was longer than the others, and only one end of it was on fire. He clamped his mouth around the other end, turned and started to walk softly to the door.

Another log fell into the space where the stick had been. A crackling noise erupted, and a shower of sparks rose up into the air. It wasn't a lot of noise. But it was enough to wake up the Skookums.

"Look," shrieked the one who had brought Coyote inside. "It's Coyote, and he's escaping with our fire!" They jumped up and rushed to the door. If the opening hadn't been so small, and if they hadn't all tried to push through at once, they might have caught him. They were only stuck in the doorway for a moment, but that was long enough for Coyote to escape.

The snow had stopped and the moon shone brightly down. Coyote raced toward the woods far below him. The wet patches on the trail had turned to ice, and he slipped again and again. The Skookums gained on him. Just when he thought that he couldn't run any farther, he heard a shrill cry from above. Eagle was swooping down toward him. "Throw the stick into the air! I'll catch it." Coyote flung his head backward, opening his mouth to let go of the stick. It circled upward, and Eagle grabbed it in his talons.

The Skookums were so close that they could nearly grab Coyote. But when they saw Eagle flying away with the fire, they leapt into the air, using their spirit powers to fly after him.

Coyote's tail was in flames. He dropped and rolled in

the snow. The fire in his tail sizzled and died. He was all matted and dirty, and there were scorch marks along his once-fluffy, beautiful tail.

Eagle soared into the sky, hoping that the Skookums wouldn't be able to fly as high or as fast as he could. But they could, and they did. Their shrieking voices came closer and closer. He made tight circles, and he plunged toward the ground, veering upward at the last possible moment, trying to lose them. But they circled and plunged and veered as well as he did.

There's nothing I can do except fly as quickly as possible toward the forest and hope that Mountain Lion is waiting for me, Eagle thought. And he headed straight toward the treeline.

Mountain Lion was there, and when he saw that the Skookums had nearly overtaken Eagle, he roared out: "Drop the fire, Eagle. I'll catch it."

Eagle did, and as it dropped toward the ground, one of the Skookums shot past the great bird. She was about to close her hand on the branch when Mountain Lion leapt high into the air, grabbed the stick in his teeth, twisted his body, landed lightly on the ground and bounded into the forest.

Mountain Lion could run much faster than Coyote, and soon the voices of the angry Skookums were far behind him. But there was a problem. The fierce animal couldn't run that fast for very long. Soon he began to slow down, and the shrieks of the Skookums became louder and closer.

Just when it seemed that they were about to overtake him, Mountain Lion arrived at the bush-filled part of the forest. Squirrel sat on a low branch, chirring and scolding. "Quickly, Lion," she chattered. "Climb up the tree and give me the fire."

"I'm exhausted," Mountain Lion muttered between his teeth. "You'll have to come and get it."

Squirrel raced down the trunk of the tree and grabbed the stick. By this time it had burned down to a small stub. The Skookums rushed at her as she scurried back up, and they nearly caught her tail.

Filled with fear, Squirrel ran along a branch and hurled herself into the air. It was a long jump, and she just managed to clutch the end of another branch. Again and again, she leapt dangerously from tree to tree. Each time Squirrel reached the thicker part of a branch, she would turn her head over her shoulder to see how close the Skookums were. When she turned, the flame touched against her back and she had to curl her tail upward and twitch it to beat out sparks that landed on her fur. To this day, when squirrels sit on a branch, their tails curl up against their backs and twitch.

She arrived at the clearing, where she found Chipmunk timidly looking out from behind an old fallen log. "Here," she trilled, "catch the fire." She dropped the stick, which had burned down to almost nothing. Chipmunk grabbed it and scurried along, beside, under and through old and rotting logs toward the pond where he knew Frog was waiting.

Before he reached the water, Chipmunk had to cross a clearing. There were no logs or fallen branches to protect him. When he dashed into the open, one of the Skookums reached out and caught him. Chipmunk squirmed and wiggled his way free, but the sharp nails of the Skookum left scratch lines down his back. The stripes that chipmunks wear today are reminders of those scratches.

"Throw it in my mouth! Throw it in my mouth!" Frog croaked as Chipmunk rushed up. By this time, the fire wasn't much more than a burning coal. Chipmunk did as he was told. Frog clamped his mouth shut and turned to plunge into the pond.

But he couldn't. The youngest Skookum stamped her foot on his tail. Frog pulled so hard against her that his tail broke loose. Free, he dove to the mud at the bottom of the pond. The stump of his tail hurt terribly. To this day, frogs lose their tails when they grow up, a reminder of what happened to Frog long ago.

The Skookums stopped at the edge of the water. They could run. They could fly. They could leap from branch to branch. But they couldn't swim. "If we wait long enough," the oldest said to the others, "Frog will have to come up for air, and then we can get him."

But Frog could hold his breath much longer than they realized. He moved slowly through the mud to the opposite side of the pool, near where a willow tree leaned its branches over the water. Then he sat there, knowing that the Skookums would probably get tired of waiting for him and fall asleep.

They did.

But when they heard a rippling noise from across the pond, they woke up quickly. They saw Frog's head just above the water, right near the willow tree on the bank.

They gave a mighty leap across the pool. But not before Frog had opened his mouth and spat the burning coal into the bark of the willow tree.

The Skookums rushed at the tree, shrieking with anger. They demanded that the willow tree give up the fire. When that didn't happen, they threatened to destroy it. They shook its branches, beat on its trunk and ripped away some of the bark. Finally, they gave up and decided to go back home. They still had fire at home, but if they didn't feed it some wood, soon it would go out. They turned away from the pond, walked across the clearing and disappeared into the forest.

The villagers came out of their houses and gathered around the willow tree. Frog hopped out of the water to join them. Chipmunk and Squirrel scurried over to the tree. Soon Mountain Lion bounded from the forest, and Eagle soared down from the sky. They all gazed at the tree with puzzled looks on their faces.

"We've got the fire now," the people remarked. "But what good is it to us in the willow tree?"

They sat silently, despondently. Then they heard a voice from the edge of the clearing. "Why are you all standing around that tree? Why aren't you in your homes enjoying the fire, feeling warm, and cooking food?" It was Coyote, still looking scruffy and wet and with burn marks on what had been his beautiful fluffy tail.

He trotted up to the group, listened as they explained their new problem and then lay down to think. After a while, he stood up and began to bark out orders. "We'll need someone to gather tufts of grass, someone else to find some wood chips made by the beavers, and someone to get small twigs, lots of them. And make sure everything is very dry."

At this time of year, nearly everything was wet, so it took a lot of time and careful searching. Finally, Coyote looked at the piles of grass, wood chips and twigs and said, "That's enough."

"Now I will show you how to get the fire out of the tree," Coyote told the animals. He broke off a dead willow branch, cut a flat side to it and then made a small hole in the flat side. He took a much smaller branch, made a point on one end and then arranged some of the dried grass along the branch. Then he placed the stick in the hole and began to whirl it back and forth very quickly. After what seemed like a very long time, a wisp of smoke rose from the hole. "Push a few pieces of grass nearer to the hole," Coyote told the people. "Do it as gently as you can. And then blow on the grass very, very gently."

When they blew, a tiny flame burst up from the grass. Soon, all of it was on fire. Coyote ordered the people to lay the smallest twigs very carefully over the flames. When these started to burn, he told them to put some of the wood chips on.

Soon a small fire was burning vigorously. Coyote told the villagers to add large logs to keep the flames from going out. Then he told the villagers to collect more grass, chips, twigs and logs to take to each house.

While a few people stayed near the willow tree to keep the fire going, Coyote showed the villagers how to build pits in the middle of their homes, how to line the pits with stones and then how to make small holes at the peaks of their roofs. When they had done this, he showed them how to arrange the grass, twigs, chips and logs in the pit. Soon, all the people had fires burning in their homes.

The winter turned out to be the best one anyone in the village had ever experienced. Nearly all of the young, old and sick people lived to welcome the arrival of spring. Everyone enjoyed the light and the warmth of the fire, and they particularly liked their warm acorn soup and their cooked salmon.

All of this happened long, long ago. Now, when the Araar see a coyote with its scruffy tail and burn marks, a squirrel with its bushy tail pressed against its back, a chipmunk with dark stripes on its back, and a frog with no tail, they remember how the people first got fire. More important, they remember that, through co-operation, the people were able to accomplish a task that seemed almost impossible.

COYOTE

CATCHES FIRE

UNiTED STATES

:: Stories about Coyote are found in many Native groups on the prairies and west coast. Sometimes he was clever and sometimes foolish. Sometimes he was helpful and sometimes selfish. His actions gave listeners examples of good and bad behaviour. In this tale from Zuni Pueblo in New Mexico, everything Coyote does violates the people's belief in community harmony.

Coyote loved to catch things. You could say he went on quests to catch things.

One time he was trotting across the desert when he spied a monarch butterfly ahead of him. *I think I'd like to catch it,* he thought to himself. Why he wanted to catch it and what he would do with it never entered his mind.

Coyote began to trot faster, but the butterfly kept ahead of him. He ran until he was just behind the orange-and-black flutterer. He leapt into the air, but the butterfly was too high, and Coyote landed on a small patch of hedgehog cactus. The spikes of the cactus caught in his feet, and he had to pull them out with his teeth before he could limp home.

Another time, a very pretty girl in the pueblo caught his eye. *I would like to talk to her. When she sees how handsome I am, she will want to give me a kiss.* He ran toward her. The very pretty girl saw him coming, and she ran too, all the way to her home. She disappeared through the low doorway. Just as Coyote arrived, the very pretty girl's brother came out. He was very big, and he didn't look very happy. Coyote caught it that time.

On another occasion, Coyote was walking along, enjoying the early morning sunshine. It had been cloudy and rainy during the last few days, and he was happy to see bright blue sky again. The only thing he wanted to catch was a few rays before it got too hot. As he walked by a low mesa, something caught his eye. Curious, he trotted closer to see what it was. A group of crows had lined up to practise for a ceremony in the village. Coyote was very impressed by the way that they all moved together. He started tapping his foot to the sound of the drum one of the crows was playing. *That's a very catchy beat*, he thought to himself.

Then Coyote had an idea. The people of the village never took much notice of him. Perhaps if the crows would let him join their dance, he would catch the villagers' attention. They would be very impressed. Then he would feel very important.

"Brother crows," he called out very politely. "You are such wonderful dancers. Would you teach me your dance?"

The crows knew that Coyote could be a real nuisance, but, because they were polite, they allowed him to join them. "You must remember," the leader told him very sternly, "this is a very dignified dance. We practise very hard so that we will all be in time with each other. Pay attention, and do exactly what you see the others doing."

Coyote agreed. He tried very hard to follow the intricate steps of the other dancers. But he just couldn't catch on. He became discouraged, and then he became bored. *This is a dull dance, anyway. I think I'll make up my own dance*, he thought to himself. He began to caper around, jumping in and out of the line of crows. He didn't bother to keep in step. Then he bounded to the front of the line, ahead of the leader and made up his own dance.

He jumped high in the air and flipped backward. He walked on his front paws. He spun around and around until he became dizzy. Then he leaned against a large boulder, catching his breath and regaining his balance.

The crows continued to practise, but the glint in their eyes showed that they were becoming very angry and impatient with this dancer who wouldn't keep in time, who wouldn't follow the leader and who wouldn't be a member of the group.

They reached one edge of the mesa, turned around and started dancing back, moving their legs more quickly and flapping their wings. When they came near to the other edge of the mesa, they began to beat their wings harder and harder. Then each crow launched himself into the air. They flew in a circle, landed gracefully back on the mesa and once again formed a straight line.

Coyote was filled with amazement and admiration. They flew so beautifully. He decided that he didn't just want to be able to dance like the crows. He wanted to be able to fly like they did. That would certainly catch the attention of the villagers. Maybe then the very pretty girl would want to talk to him.

He trotted along beside the crow leader as the dancers moved toward the other end of the mesa. "You fly so beautifully. Watching you was so wonderful. I wish I could fly like you. I didn't do too well dancing, but I'm sure I'd be a much better flyer. Please, won't you teach me how? I promise that I will do as you say."

"But you don't have wings, Coyote. How could you possibly fly?" the leader replied with scorn in his voice.

Coyote pleaded, "There must be something you can do. If I can't learn to fly, I will be unhappy for the rest of my life."

"Sit over there, Coyote, and wait until we have finished practising our dance. Then I will talk with the other crows. If we put our ideas together, we may be able to come up with a way for you to fly." The leader was very stern, so Coyote walked to another part of the mesa and waited very impatiently.

The practice over, the crows gathered in a circle. Coyote couldn't hear what they were saying to each other, but he was sure that he heard some laughter.

Soon the leader came back to where he was sitting and fidgeting. "If you will do exactly as you are told, each of us will give you one of our feathers. Then we will teach you to fly."

Coyote was so excited that he jumped up, did a backflip and started to spin in circles. "Sit down," the leader commanded. Then he called one of the crows forward and told him to pull a feather out of his wing. He took the feather and, commanding Coyote to put one of his legs forward, shoved the feather into a muscle. It hurt dreadfully, but Coyote didn't whimper.

One by one, the other crows came forward. Each pulled out a wing feather with his beak and then stuck it into one of Coyote's legs. It hurt so much that several times, the foolish animal wanted to tell the crows to stop. But when he thought about how amazed the villagers would be when they saw him fly into the village, he said nothing. Soon there were feathers on the back of each of his front legs and all along the sides of his body.

"You go to the back of the line, Coyote," the leader ordered. "Then we will all go to one side of the mesa and start running the other way, flapping our wings. You must keep up, and you must make sure you don't stop beating your wings."

Coyote agreed. "Thank you," he said. "I can't wait to fly back to the village."

Coyote took his place and began running. He was going pretty fast.

"Start flapping your wings now, Coyote," the chief called out over his shoulder.

Coyote tried. But his wings were really his front legs. Every time he tried to lift them, he fell face first into the dust. He tried hard—so hard, in fact—that he didn't notice that he was coming to the edge of the mesa. From high in the air came the command: "Stop, Coyote! You're going to fall off." He skidded to a stop, sat down and looked enviously upward at the circling crows.

The crows landed, and once again they gathered together, chuckling to each other as they discussed what they should do about Coyote. Finally, the leader approached the miserable coyote. "If you want to be able to fly, you'll have to learn to take off. You can't do that without flapping your wings . . . I mean your legs. We think that you'd better start running on your hind legs only. That way your front legs will be free to flap. Start practising, and we'll be back."

Then he led his band off into the air, where they performed lazy loops.

Coyote started running on his hind legs. He lost his balance and landed on his chin, scraping it very badly. Then he tried again and landed on his stomach, knocking all the wind out of himself. But he didn't give up. He desperately wanted to impress the people of the village, particularly the very pretty girl.

Finally, he seemed to get the hang of it. He didn't trip or fall, and if he beat his arms fast enough, he could almost feel his back feet lifting off the ground. The crows landed. The leader walked up to him and said, "You're ready, Coyote. Stay at the end of the line, do what everyone else is doing, and you'll be fine."

Coyote did as he was told and followed the birds across the mesa, beating his wings furiously. When he came to the edge, he gave a push with his hind legs, launched out into the air and started falling.

High above, the crows shouted encouragement, "Don't stop, Coyote! Beat your wings harder and faster."

He did what he was told. His arms ached. The air coming into his lungs felt like it was burning. But he gradually began to rise.

When he reached the crows circling in the sky, he took his place at the end of the group. He felt very pleased with himself and smiled when he heard the flock cheering him.

Coyote followed the birds ahead of him, doing what they did, following the leader. It felt wonderful to be a member of the crow family, circling and gliding, feeling the air under his wings.

But, after a while, Coyote started to get bored. *Why do we have to keep doing the same circles and glides?*

Why can't we do something different, something new and exciting? After two more circles, he made a decision. He wouldn't stay with the birds. He'd fly high into the sky, just like an eagle.

If he'd just gone off by himself, it would have been bad enough. But he couldn't resist calling back to the crows. "You stodgy old birds, just doing the same thing over and over. You have no sense of adventure. Only I can soar high, high into the sky."

Higher and higher he went. Down below, the mesa seemed like a very small circle in the desert. Turning to his left, he could see the pueblo, looking very tiny in the distance. *I think I'll fly over to the village and land at the plaza. That will certainly catch the eye of the very pretty girl. But first, I'll go a little higher.*

What Coyote didn't know was that the crows could fly as high as he could, higher in fact. They had been pretty annoyed with him since his show-off dancing. But when he insulted them and flew out of the circle, they became very angry. "I think it's time we taught this foolish Coyote a lesson," the leader called to the other crows. "Follow me." He broke from the circle and headed upward toward Coyote.

Coyote was so busy enjoying gliding on the updraft of air he had caught, and so happy thinking about the wonderful reception he expected when he came to the village, that he didn't notice the crows approaching. Suddenly, he felt a jerk just below one of his elbows. He turned his head to see the leader pulling out a feather and placing it back in his own wing.

He started to say "Ouch! That hurts!" But before he

could get all the words out, he felt another tug just below the other elbow. Another of the crows had pulled out a feather and stuck it back in his own wing.

And another . . . and another . . . and another . . . until the crows had taken back all the feathers they had given him.

Coyote kept gliding for a few seconds, and then he started to fall. He beat his arms frantically and cried out, "Please help me! I'm going to hurt myself! I might die!" But the crows ignored him and flew away.

Coyote had flown so high that he had a long way to fall. He dropped faster and faster. In fact, before he was halfway to the ground, he was going so fast that his tail began to smoulder. It was glowing like a meteorite because of the friction in the air. If it had been dark, and the people of the pueblo had been looking at the sky, they might have thought Coyote was a shooting star.

By the time that Coyote had neared the ground, his tail had caught fire. He landed with a terrible thud. How it was that he wasn't killed, or at the least that he didn't break all the bones in his body, no one knows to this day. Perhaps it was because he landed on a large patch of very spongy and very sharp cactuses. In any case, he jumped right up and started to run about, trying to escape the flame at the tip of his tail. But his running only made the fire burn more brightly and fiercely.

Luckily for him, there was a pool just ahead. He was so desperate with pain that he didn't see it. He tripped on a rock and belly-flopped into the water with a great splash. The fire on his tail stopped burning. He stayed in the muddy water until the sun began to set and then crawled out. His tail was burned. His body was bruised. And his skin still smarted from where the feathers used to be. Exhausted, he lay on the ground. In a few minutes, he fell asleep.

As often happens at night in the desert, it became very cold. Coyote shivered so much that he woke himself up several times. Just before dawn, he started sneezing so violently that he couldn't get back to sleep.

Every muscle of his body was sore. He had a headache. He had a fever. There were red marks on his fur where the cactus spikes had pricked him and where the feathers had been removed. *I must get back to my home before anyone sees me*, he thought to himself.

He'd just reached his part of the pueblo when he started coughing very loudly. Some of the people came to their doors to see what the matter was. He tried to sneak along through the shadows, but his movement caught people's attention.

"Look at that miserable Coyote, all muddy and dirty. What ever happened to you, Coyote?"

Coyote answered with an enormous sneeze.

Someone laughed very loudly and called out, "Why Coyote's been out hunting early in the morning and he's caught a cold!"

MAUI

FINDS FIRE—TWICE

NEW ZEALAND

:: From New Zealand to Hawaii, traditional Polynesian peoples told stories about Maui, the trickster and mischief-maker. Although he was often selfish and foolish, he sometimes used his cleverness and magic powers to help his people. One of the favourite Maui stories, the account of his quest for fire, is found in many different versions. This one comes from the Maori people of New Zealand.

When Maui was growing up, he spent much of his time playing tricks on other people. When he wasn't playing tricks, he was asking questions—a lot of them. You see, in addition to being mischievous, Maui was curious, and he was never satisfied until he found answers to the questions he asked.

One evening as he was staring into the flames of his mother's cooking fire, a question came into his mind: *Where does fire come from?* He turned to his mother and asked her. A strange look came into her eyes. She knew the answer to his question. But she didn't want to tell him. So she said, "That's not important. What's important is that we enjoy all the things that fire does for us and that we never let it die out."

The next morning, he asked his question to the other villagers. None of them knew the answer. So he returned home and asked his mother again. He kept asking her for several days, and still she wouldn't tell him. *There must be a way to find out*, Maui thought to himself. He was never a person to give up easily.

Then one night, he had an idea. It was raining very hard,

and people were busily protecting their fires from being drowned in the deluge. *Maybe,* Maui thought, *if all the fires in the village were put out, Mother would have to say where the fire came from.*

And so, late one night, Maui crept outside, gathered some water and put out one of the fires. All night, he put out fire after fire. He nearly got caught when the hiss of the water hitting the flames woke someone up. But the person turned over and went back to sleep. By the time he had put out all the fires, Maui was tired. He crept back to his hut, lay down and was snoring in seconds.

He hadn't been asleep very long when he was awoken by a shout and then heard another and another and another. He came outside rubbing his eyes. People were standing near their firepits, looking in horror and dismay at the muddy grey ashes in front of them. "What will we do now? How will we get new fire?" they asked.

Maui's mother came forward. The villagers respected her because she was very wise and always helped others with their problems. "I will tell you where to find fire and how you can get it."

She explained that fire came from her mother, Mahuika, who lived in a cave far to the north on Te Ika-a-Maui. It would be a long and dangerous journey across the Te Tai-o-Rehua Sea and into the dark cave where the old lady lived. "The person who goes to get the fire must be brave and must be very respectful to Mahuika. If she becomes angry, she certainly won't give you any fire to bring back to us, and she might burn you alive with her fire."

She looked at the people in front of her. But none of

them looked back. They stared at the ground, and they scuffed the dirt with their toes.

"I will go," a youthful voice suddenly exclaimed. The people looked toward the sound of the voice. It was Maui. They smiled. Usually they found him very annoying. Now they were glad he'd spoken up because it meant that none of them would have to make the trip. Maui was smiling, too. It wasn't just that he'd finally got an answer to his question, but also because the people were looking at him as if he were a hero. That was a nice change.

Maui's mother had a puzzled look on her face. She had suspicions about how and why the fires had gone out and why Maui had so quickly volunteered to make the dangerous journey. But she didn't say anything. Instead, she walked back to the hut with him and gave him instructions for the trip.

Maui left the village early the next morning. He trotted down the trail to the beach, found his *waka*, pushed it into the water and began to paddle north. All that day, through the night and into the next day, he paddled hard. He battled high waves that threatened to swamp the boat and winds that kept pushing him back toward home. As he passed the entrance to Raukawa, vicious currents caught the boat and began to pull it into a whirlpool. Maui paddled as hard as he could through the roiling waters and barely escaped the whirlpool. Finally, at sunset, he reached the shore of Te Ika-a-Maui. He beached his canoe, found a soft, dry spot under a nearby tree and fell into a deep sleep.

The next morning, he found a path heading inland and followed it. He passed great pools of hot steaming mud.

Ashes floated down from distant volcanoes that belched fire and foul-smelling smoke. Early in the afternoon, he found a cave. Two very large rocks flanked the entrance. *This must be the place I'm looking for,* he said to himself. *Mother told me to look for two boulders.*

Before he entered the cave, Maui cut a long thin pole out of a sapling he found not far from the cave. *It will probably be pretty dark in there,* he thought. *I'll need something to feel my way. Mother said there were drop-offs and bottomless pits all along the path.*

It was very dark. In fact, it was completely dark. Maui moved slowly and carefully, touching the walls of the cave with one hand and tapping the stick on the ground ahead of him. Once, when he tapped his stick, it didn't hit anything. He threw a pebble in front of him, but he couldn't hear it land. He must be at the edge of a pit. On his hands and knees, he felt his way around it. Then he stood up and moved forward. The way twisted and turned, but it always sloped downward.

The air became warmer and warmer and then very hot. Time and again, Maui had to take his hand off the wall and wipe the sweat from his forehead. He came to a bend in the tunnel and moved cautiously around it. In the distance, he saw a light. It became brighter and brighter as he moved toward it.

In a few minutes, Maui found himself in a huge cavern. The light was coming from pools filled with fire. He looked around, and there, right across from him, sitting on what seemed to be a huge rock throne, sat a very, very large and very, very old woman.

"Who are you? Why are you here? What do you want?"
Her booming voice echoed off the cavern walls. And it
didn't sound very friendly.

It was Mahuika. "Grandmother, it is Maui, your grandson," he said in a voice that sounded respectful and a little
frightened. "My brothers put out all the fires in the village. I
have come to ask you for some more."

Mahuika ordered him to approach her. As he came
closer, he saw that her fingers and thumbs were made of
fire. Now he felt more than a little frightened. But he didn't
want his grandmother to notice.

"Before I give you fire to take back to your people, you
must help me to eat and drink. Whenever I pick up a cup
of water, the flames of my fingers turn it to steam before I
can get it to my mouth. And my food is usually burned to
cinders."

"I would be happy to help you," replied Maui, trying to
sound as polite and cheerful as he could.

After he'd helped her to eat, she pulled off one of her
flaming fingers and put it on the ground in front of him. He
sharpened the end of his stick and speared the finger with it.

"Treat it with care. My fingers are like children to me.
Make sure that no one steals it or that it doesn't fall in the
water when you're paddling home." Maui promised to be
careful and started back up the tunnel, the flaming finger
lighting his way.

When he arrived back at his canoe, his love of mischief
seemed to wake up. He doused the finger-flame in the water
and headed back to the cave. He told Mahuika that a giant
wave, the biggest he'd ever seen, had overturned his boat

and extinguished the flame. He had barely been able to hang on to the overturned waka and make his way to shore.

His grandmother told him that she was glad that he hadn't drowned, gave him another flaming finger and once more warned him to be careful.

Again the spirit of mischief seized Maui. He threw the flaming finger as far as he could into the ocean and returned to the cave, telling Mahuika that a giant eagle had seized the finger and flown off with it. Again Maui received another finger and another warning.

This happened seven more times, with seven different excuses. Each time Maui's grandmother gave him more fire and another warning. At first she seemed exasperated at Maui's carelessness. Then she became annoyed, and soon, more and more angry.

But when he returned the 10th time and only the thumb on her left hand was left, she became enraged. You might even say she blew her top. "You have lost nine of my children. You cannot have the last one."

She stood up, growing bigger and bigger. The flame in the pools around her burned more fiercely, shooting up to the roof of the cavern, through an opening and up into the sky. People living far from the cave could see flames and smoke. "That must be a new volcano," they said to each other.

In the cavern, Mahuika pointed her thumb at Maui, and an enormous flame roared toward him. He turned and fled up the tunnel, the flame following.

He reached the entrance to the cave and ran outside. The flame followed. Suddenly a great wind sprung up, scattering the flame across the land. He could hear his grandmother coming up the tunnel, shrieking, "You must be punished!"

Maui stumbled and crawled toward the seashore, his eyes stinging and his skin drenched in sweat. It seemed as if the world were on fire. When he got to the water's edge, his canoe was engulfed in flames. Behind him, his grandmother's voiced boomed. She was coming closer and closer.

He felt really frightened—terrified, in fact—for the first time in his life. His skin felt as if it were about to boil or melt. In desperation, he dove into the water and used his magical powers to turn himself into a *hoki* fish. *If I can swim deep enough, I can escape the heat and my grandmother's anger,* he thought to himself.

He went so deep that he could see no light. At first, the water was cool. But then it became warm, then very hot, and finally, it started to boil. Maui shot to the surface, and, giving his tail fins a mighty flick, he rose above the now-boiling water.

He used his magic once more and turned himself into a bird, a *kārearea*. As he shot upward, the burning ashes landed on his back and wings. They became smudged with streaks of brown and grey.

Up and up Maui flew until he was so high in the air that he could see both the North and South islands. All of Te Ika-a-Maui was in flames. Then the wind blew the fire across Raukawa, and Te Wai Pounanamu began to burn as well. Maui experienced a feeling he'd never had before—he felt guilty about something he had done. He had angered his grandmother so much that she had set the world on fire.

Because of him, his family and all the other villagers might die. *The people believed I was a hero. Now they will hate me forever,* he thought sadly to himself.

He also felt helpless. Even though he had magical powers, these great fires were more than he could deal with. In despair, he called out to the god Te Ihorangi, "Please, send rain. Do not let the world and all the people, birds, fish and animals be burned." He didn't say that he was also getting quite worried for himself.

The rain came. It poured for days. Then, just as the last flames were flickering into embers, Maui, still circling high in the sky, noticed someone moving on the shore of the South Island. It was Mahuika. She had somehow made her way to Te Wai Pounanamu, where her fires hadn't burned everything. She was holding her hand in the air, the last thumb still burning, looking for something.

With the keen sight that his falcon eyes had given him, Maui watched. He saw her walk toward a *kiakomako* tree and press her thumb against it. The flame disappeared. Maui understood. She had hidden the fire inside the tree.

She walked away from the tree, reached the shore and magically travelled back to her home on the North Island. Then Maui flew to the ground, turned himself back into a boy and walked over to the tree. He went round and round the tree, examining the trunk, the branches and the leaves. He could find no sign of the fire.

It must be in there, he thought to himself. *But that won't help the people in the village. If I don't find a way to get it out of the tree, there won't be any fire for the people back home. They won't think I'm a hero anymore. I can't go home now. I'll have to stay here. It will be lonely, but I don't want to see the looks on the faces of the villagers.*

Maui stayed near the kiakomako tree for several days, feeling lonely and very sorry for himself. One morning, he heard the sound of someone or something very large moving through the bush and small trees. His curiosity began to grow. He hid behind a clump of thick bushes and waited. The noise came closer.

It was Mahuika. Maui knew he'd better not let her find him. But, because his curiosity was getting greater and greater, he stayed where he was, peering cautiously through the leaves. His grandmother walked up to the kiakomako, broke off a branch, peeled the bark, and used a piece of broken shell to carve a point at one end. Then she walked over to a *mahoe* tree, broke off a bigger branch, and after peeling away the bark, she used the shell to gouge out a long narrow grove.

What was all this about? What was she doing? Maui wondered.

Mahuika sat on the ground, held the mahoe branch on the ground with her feet, bent over and began rubbing the kiakomako stick back and forth, very quickly, in the groove. Soon, a wisp of smoke curled up from the stick and then a small flame. Mahuika continued vigorously pushing the stick back and forth. The flame grew. After a while, one end of the mahoe stick was burning vigorously.

She held the branch to where each of her fingers and thumbs had been. The flame on the stick jumped to each of them. "I have my children back," she said in a soft and loving voice. Her lips curved into a gentle smile as she left the clearing and walked back to the beach.

Maui smiled as well. *I have found fire again*, he said to himself. *I will tell my people, and they will be very proud of me.*

After he was sure that his grandmother had returned to her home in the cavern, Maui made his way back to his village. When the people saw that he had no fire, they were very angry. "You are no hero!" they shouted. "The only thing you are any good at is making trouble and mischief."

His mother looked very sad. She had known that Maui had put out the village fires. She wanted his search for fire to be successful, and not just for the villagers. She wanted to be proud of her son and for him to feel proud of himself.

"You're right," Maui responded to the villagers. "I don't have the fire right here. I left it in a tree not far from the seashore. Come with me, and I will show you."

Everyone smiled a snickering kind of smile that showed no one believed him. People were about to return to their huts when one of them said, "Why don't we go and see? It won't take too long." He and a couple of villagers decided to make the trip with Maui back to the clearing. They still didn't believe him, but they thought it would be fun to laugh at him when he couldn't show them the fire.

When they arrived at the clearing and couldn't see any fire, the people jeered and turned to go back home. "Don't leave just yet," Maui called, "I'll show you the fire." He broke off the two branches and made the point and groove just the way that he'd seen Mahuika do. The people looked at him, shook their heads and exchanged knowing smiles.

Maui began rubbing the kiakomako stick in the groove of the mahoe branch. For a few minutes, nothing happened.

The villagers got restless, bored and annoyed. "Let's go home," one of them muttered angrily.

"Not yet," Maui said, "just a little longer." So they stayed. They would have a really good laugh when Maui couldn't show them any fire.

Then the smoke and the tiny flame appeared, and soon the entire mahoe branch was on fire. "When the rain started, I put the fire here to keep it safe. Wasn't it a clever idea?" he said, a sly grin on his face. Everyone was really amazed. They cheered and congratulated Maui. He was very pleased with himself.

"We will take this burning branch back home," he told them. "And I will use my magic to put the fire into the kia-komako trees around the village. Then, whenever people's fires go out, they can just go to the trees to get some more. No long trips to visit my grandmother."

The people never found out that Maui had put out the village fires, that he had angered his grandmother so much that she had nearly destroyed the world, or that he hadn't really come up with the idea of putting fire in the wood of the tree.

Everyone was very happy with him. And that made him happy. *Why let out the secrets and cause a lot of trouble for myself?* he smiled to himself.

CANADA AND THE UNiTED STATES :: The

Anishnabeg (Ojibway/Chippewa) who lived around Lake Superior often told stories about Nanabozho. Although he loved to play tricks, Nanabozho sometimes used his cleverness and spirit powers to help the people. This story takes place at a time when the people did not have fire and the leaves did not turn bright colours in the autumn.

anabozho stepped outside his wigwam, took a deep breath of the cold morning air and then slowly let it out, watching the little cloud that formed. The ground in front of him was green and silver. During the night, frost had formed on some of the maple leaves that had fallen. A cold breeze from the north rustled the few leaves that still clung to the branches. The pale light of the sun shone through the nearly bare trees.

It is going to be a beautiful day, he thought to himself. *It's going to be cold. But it will be dry and bright and sunny. It will be a good day to go hunting. There may be a few ducks or geese resting on the pond. But first, I must say good morning to Nokomis.*

He went over to his grandmother's wigwam and called out, "Good morning, Nokomis. It is going to be a fine day."

"Come in, you mischief-maker, you," she answered in a voice that seemed to tremble. She loved her grandson, but she knew that the tricks he played often made the other people in the village very annoyed.

"Grandmother," the young man said when he came inside, "what is the matter?" The old woman had a fur robe wrapped tightly around her. She was shivering, and in the dim light, her lips looked almost blue.

"It may be a nice day for you, Little Rabbit," Nokomis answered, using her favourite name for her grandson. "But it isn't for me. Now that the sun is low in the sky and the cold winds have started coming across the Gichigami, I can't keep warm, and I can't eat. In the morning my food is frozen. I don't have many teeth left, and I can't chew the meat."

Nanabozho was startled. He didn't often think about other people, and he hadn't considered that it wasn't a beautiful autumn day for his grandmother. Now he understood how she felt, but he didn't know how to help her. "I don't know what to do, Nokomis. Isn't there something I can do to make you feel warmer and make your food easier to chew?"

"There might be something. I have heard that long ago, the people had something called fire. It made them warm. It helped them to soften their food, and it gave them light during the long winter nights. But then it was stolen by an old man with great spirit powers. He took it to his wigwam far away across the Gichigami. Many people went to him to ask for some of the fire. But none of them ever came back. No one has tried for a long, long time. People say that he is still alive. He is old, but he never gets older. He lives with his two daughters, who always stay young and beautiful."

"I think that I will cross the Gichigami and get the fire for you," Nanabozho told his grandmother. He wanted to help her, and he liked the idea of meeting two girls who were always young and beautiful. Nokomis tried to stop him, telling him that crossing the great lake would be too dangerous at this time of year. And even if he did make it to the other side, the old man might kill him.

But Nanabozho had made up his mind. He left the village and trotted along the trail to Munising Bay, where he kept his canoe. When he reached the shore, the sun had disappeared behind low, grey clouds, and the breeze had turned into a strong north wind. Beyond the channel that ran between Gichiminising, the big island, and Ishpabecca, the great cliffs, he could see whitecaps. But he didn't turn back. He was excited by the idea of a new adventure. He wanted to help his grandmother. And, of course, he wanted to see the two young and beautiful girls.

The trip across the Gichigami was difficult and dangerous. It began to rain as he was leaving the shore, and once he reached the open lake, the rain turned to sleet. The air became colder and colder, and the waves higher and higher. It was all he could do to keep his canoe moving forward and to keep the waves from swamping it. The sleet and the water splashed over him, freezing his eyelashes and his buckskins.

Only his determination to help his grandmother, his courage, his strength and his skill, along with the possibility that he might see two young and beautiful girls, kept him going. He paddled all day and through the night, struggling to keep the nose of his canoe facing into the north wind.

Finally, in the middle of the next day, he reached the north shore of the big lake. He stepped into the frigid, knee-deep water, pulled his canoe up high onto the sand and gravel, and turned it over. He sat down to rest his sore muscles and began to chew a nearly frozen strip of meat he'd brought with him. *I see what Nokomis means,* he thought as he gnawed at his very tough meal.

Then Nanabozho stood up and looked toward the forest. He spotted a trail. He didn't know where he should look for the old man's wigwam and decided that following the path was as good a plan as any. He moved quietly through the forest until he reached a clearing with a very large wigwam in the middle of it. From a hole in the roof, small clouds, like the clouds of his breath on a frosty morning, rose upward.

Perhaps this has something to do with fire, he thought. *But how can I get inside to find out? If the old man has such great spirit power, he'll discover me right away.*

Nanabozho leaned against a tree and began to think about how to enter the wigwam. Each idea he came up with had something wrong with it. As the afternoon wore on, the sun broke through the clouds. But it didn't have much warmth to it. He realized that it would be very cold when night came. *I hope I can find a way to get inside before dark. If Nokomis is right, the fire will keep me warm.*

After the sun set, Nanabozho began to shiver. His teeth chattered. What was he to do? Not only did it seem that he would fail to bring fire back to his grandmother, but also that he would freeze to death before morning.

He heard voices coming from the wigwam. He couldn't hear the words, but it sounded like young women talking— maybe beautiful young women.

Then another voice boomed out. It was a man's voice, and Nanabozho had no trouble hearing it. "You girls are getting lazy. You haven't brought any wood inside since this morning. If you want to stay warm tonight and have something warm to eat tomorrow morning, you'd better go out and get some wood right now. And don't rescue any little animals or birds and bring them back with you. That squirrel you found this morning died, and I had to throw it into the cooking pot."

Now Nanabozho knew how to get into the wigwam. Using his own spirit powers, he turned himself into a little rabbit. He hopped to a muddy puddle that hadn't frozen over, rolled in it and then hopped toward the woodpile, shivering as violently as he could. He was as miserable-looking a rabbit as he could make himself.

His plan worked perfectly. When the two beautiful young daughters came outside, one of them was carrying a lighted stick of fire so that they could find their way to the woodpile. The youngest, and most beautiful, was the first to notice the wet, muddy, shivering rabbit. She scooped him into her arms. "You get the wood. I'll take this poor little creature inside to get warm." She kissed the shivering rabbit on the nose.

When her sister, who was annoyed that she'd have to carry the wet wood, warned her that their father would be angry, the youngest one replied, "Don't worry. Father always complains, but he always lets us keep the animals."

The old man grumbled when he saw the rabbit. But he let the beautiful, youngest daughter put the rabbit close to the fire so that it could warm up. In a few minutes, the rabbit stopped shivering.

This is so much better than just wrapping myself in fur robes to keep warm, Nanabozho thought.

He watched as the older daughter put on a pair of fur mittens and picked up a rock that was resting close to the flames. When she put it in a bark pot filled with water, the rock sizzled, and steam rose into the air. She put two more rocks into the pot and then threw a handful of leaves and some chunks of meat into the water.

Soon Nanabozho smelled delicious aromas coming from the cooking pot, and he began to feel very hungry. But he knew he couldn't try to get anything to eat because the old man and his two beautiful daughters would discover him.

"Would you like some soup, grandfather?" the oldest daughter said to the old man. He nodded his head, and she scooped some out into a smaller bowl. He took a wooden spoon from a box beside him and scooped up the warm broth and tender meat. "This is very good, my daughter," he told her.

Nanabozho thought to himself, *I will have to remember what the girl did and tell Nokomis when I bring the fire to her. I know she will want to make this delicious soup.*

Gradually, Nanabozho's eyes started to close. He tried hard to stay awake, but it had been a long and difficult couple of days, and soon he was asleep.

He didn't know how long he had been sleeping, but he woke up when the old man started snoring. *Now's my chance*, he thought. Using his spirit power, he changed himself back into a young Anishnabeg man, grabbed a burning stick and turned to leave the wigwam. *It's too bad that the beautiful young daughters won't be able to see how handsome I am as a human.*

Just then the old man woke up. He'd been disturbed

by the spirit power that Nanabozho had used to transform himself. He saw Nanabozho leaving the wigwam. "Quickly girls! A young warrior has stolen fire! Chase him! I will use my spirit powers to slow him down."

Nanabozho raced across the clearing and into the forest. He could hear the girls behind him and thought, *I'll get away from them without much trouble.* He held the burning branch high above his head to light his way.

He had not been running long when he saw a clearing ahead. *I don't remember seeing this clearing on my way here,* he thought to himself. Suddenly, the ground began to heave, and a mountain of boulders rose out of the ground and covered the clearing.

Nanabozho started to climb. But as he scrambled upward, he realized that escape wouldn't be easy. The rocks were covered with ice. He had to grip the flaming stick with one hand, and when he reached upward with his other hand, it would sometimes slip off the rock, and he would fall backward on the icy boulders below. Luckily, the young and beautiful daughters were having the same trouble with the icy slope. He continued to struggle, and gradually he reached the top of the hill, slid down the other side and began running again.

Soon the light from the flaming stick shone on another clearing. *I don't remember this one either. But at least there aren't any icy boulders here.* He took a few steps and then started to sink. The dead grasses covered a muddy bog. He was up to his knees when he stopped sinking. Slowly, holding the torch as high as he could, he used his other hand to pull one leg out of the muck and place it in front of him. He pushed down until the first leg stopped sinking, and then he dragged the other leg forward.

He could hear the beautiful young daughters shouting from the edge of the clearing, telling him to turn back and give them the fire stick. Nanabozho kept struggling forward. The daughters also began to sink as they tried to cross the bog.

Nanabozho reached the edge of the bog and pulled himself onto firm, dry ground. Not far ahead, he could hear the waves of the Gichigami. He raced down the trail and came out onto the beach just as the rays of the sun began to sparkle on the water. He turned his canoe right-side up and, holding the burning brand tightly in one hand, he used the other to push the craft into the water.

He clamped the fire stick between his knees and used both hands to paddle against the currents that were pushing him back toward the shore. By now, the girls had gotten through the bog and were running along the trail. Their voices were getting closer and closer.

By the time they reached the shore, Nanabozho had paddled into deep water, and the currents had disappeared. The two young and beautiful daughters rushed into the water but stopped when it reached their knees. "You are safe now, you evil little rabbit," they called. "We can't swim, and our father's power cannot cross over the big water."

Nanabozho waved and called out, "Thank you for the gift. And I want you to know that what my grandmother Nokomis told me is right. You are both young and beautiful." Then he started paddling south.

Crossing the water was much easier this time. There was no snow and sleet, and the wind blew gently at his back. The sun rose in the sky, and the air became warmer. The wind pushed the light canoe forward. All Nanabozho had to do was steer with his paddle.

He reached Munising Bay late in the afternoon, stepped out of the canoe, and, with the brand held high, walked to the top of the gently sloping beach. He pushed the stick into the sand and returned to the shoreline to pull the canoe out of the water and turn it over. Grabbing the flaming branch, he walked along the shore until he reached the path that led to his village.

The sun had set before he reached home. When he looked up to see if the moon had risen, he saw something very strange. The strong winds of yesterday had not blown all the leaves from the trees. Those that still clung to the branches were not green. They had turned yellow and orange and red in the reflected light from the stick of fire he was carrying.

That looks very pretty, he thought to himself. *Next year, just before the leaves start to fall, I will use my spirit powers to turn them all bright colours. I will tell the people that I did it because of the fire. That way, every year when the leaves look like fire, they will remember my great adventure and the wonderful gift I brought to them.*

By the time he reached the village, the flames had burned nearly all of the stick. He quickly gathered some branches and lit them. Then he called out, "Come, everyone, and see the wonderful gift I have for you." The people were amazed as the branches caught fire and sparks flew into the sky.

Nokomis came out of her wigwam and walked very slowly toward him, a look of joy on her face. "It is a wonderful gift, Nanabozho," she said as she wrapped her frail arms around him and gave him a hug. "But the greatest gift is that you are home safely. I have been terribly worried."

After he had shown the people how to keep the fire going, he took a small stick and a few little branches into his grandmother's lodge. He made a small hole in her roof, and then he built a fire. He spread some fur robes in front of it and helped his grandmother sit down.

She held her hands toward the flames. "I feel warm again," she murmured.

He told her about his long journey. He did not exaggerate the way he would tomorrow, when he recounted the adventures to the villagers. After he told his story, he described the delicious broth he had seen the girls make. "I will make some for you tomorrow," he said.

Then he sat quietly, watching the flames and the wisps of smoke that crept up to the hole in the roof. "What is the matter, my grandson?" Nokomis finally asked.

"I have been remembering something that happened on the adventure, something I forgot to tell you. When I had turned myself into a rabbit and the beautiful youngest daughter picked me up, she kissed my nose. Of course, I couldn't kiss her back. I was just a little rabbit, and I didn't want to be discovered. And when I turned back into myself, I had to run very quickly to escape with the fire. I didn't have a chance to kiss her goodbye. But she was very beautiful. Maybe I should go back again. This time, I wouldn't have to change myself into a rabbit. Her old father knows how great my spirit powers are, and I think he might be a little afraid of me. And the youngest daughter, when she sees how handsome I am . . . "

His voice trailed off, and a dreamy smile spread across his face. Nokomis shook her head, but she smiled too.

VASILISA
AND THE BABA YAGA'S FIRE

RUSSIA :: All around the world, people tell stories about a beautiful and kind girl who is treated badly by her stepmother and stepsisters. In this Russian story, the heroine not only deals with the bad people with whom she lives, but she also travels through a dangerous forest to the home of the Baba Yaga, who is a cannibal and a witch.

The first eight years of Vasilisa's life were happy. Her family didn't have much money and their house was small, but they were rich in love.

Then, one autumn, shortly after Vasilisa's eighth birthday, her mother died. The next spring, her father remarried. Vasilisa's new stepmother and her two children were very polite and friendly when her father was in the house, but they were cruel and spiteful toward her when he was away.

Two years later, Vasilisa's father took sick and died. After that, her stepsisters treated her like a servant and made her do all the household chores. They spoke meanly and savagely to her whenever they were displeased, and they made her sleep on a straw mattress and a pile of rags in the corner of the kitchen. "The bedroom is too small for the three of us," they told her.

The stepmother hated Vasilisa, who was prettier, more clever and more good-natured than her daughters, and who was loved by all the people in the village.

After a few years, the woman decided to move to a house that was close to the deep, dark woods. It had three bedrooms. She and her two daughters could each have their own rooms, but Vasilisa would have to sleep in a corner of the kitchen.

Because the stepsisters were very selfish and spent most of the time thinking only about themselves, neither wondered how Vasilisa was able to get so much work done every day. What they didn't know was that their stepsister had help. In fact, she'd had help since the day her mother died: a doll.

A few hours before her death, Vasilisa's mother had called the girl to her. "My child," she whispered to Vasilisa, "go to my sewing basket and bring what you find under the wool and pieces of cloth."

The girl discovered a small, plain doll made of cloth. "I have made this doll for you. I put my blessings and all my love for you in it," her mother whispered. "It does not look very special, but it has special powers. When your life feels almost too much to bear, feed it a little bit of your food. It will listen to all your troubles and will help you and give you advice. But you must tell no one about it."

After her mother and father had died, whenever the stepmother and stepsisters began to treat her cruelly, she would feed the doll and pour out her sadness and grief. When she asked the doll how she would be able to do all the tasks that she had to perform, the doll told her not to worry, that she would have help. The selfish sisters and their mother never noticed that most of the chores had been completed early every morning.

As Vasilisa grew older, all the young men in the village paid attention to her. It wasn't just that she had become more and more beautiful. It was also because she was so sweet and good-natured. None of the young men paid attention to her stepsisters.

Their mother had always wanted to see her girls well married—which to her meant someone with a great deal of money. But as long as the young men were all courting Vasilisa, the mother's wish for her daughters would not come true. *If only Vasilisa weren't around,* the stepmother thought, *things would be so much better for my girls.*

She began thinking . . . and plotting.

One cold November night, the three girls sat around the table sewing. A small candle flickered in front of them, and a fire burned low in the grate. A half moon shone through the window, which was beginning to frost up from the cold. Outside, the wind howled mournfully through the bare branches of the birch trees and rattled the window.

"Vasilisa," the stepmother commanded in her sternest voice, "it is going to get very cold. You must go outside and bring us enough wood to last through the night. Be quick about it."

Obediently, Vasilia stood up, crossed the room and opened the door. A gust of wind slammed the door shut behind her. She gathered an armful of small logs and then staggered back inside with her heavy load. The room was almost completely dark. The candle was out, and there weren't even embers in the fireplace.

"You foolish girl," the stepmother hissed. "You opened the door so wide that the wind blew out the candle flame and the fire. What are we to do? We can't do our work, and we won't be able to cook anything. There is only one thing to do. You must go through the forest to the home of the Baba Yaga and bring some of her fire home to us. There's enough moonlight for you to be able to follow the pathway. You should easily be back by the time the sun sets tomorrow."

It wasn't Vasilisa's fault that the fires had gone out. The stepmother had put out the candles and the fire while Vasilisa was outside. She had wanted an excuse to send the girl she hated so much to a certain death. She expected her to be eaten up by the Baba Yaga. The powerful and evil witch had a tremendous appetite, especially for human beings. *I'll relight the fire and candles as soon as the wretched girl has left,* the stepmother thought to herself.

Although Vasilisa was terrified, she did as she was told. She felt her way to her straw bed in the corner and bent over to pick up the shawl that she used as an extra blanket. It was so dark that no one noticed that she also picked up a small doll hidden under the frayed mattress. She reached into her pocket, fed the doll the small piece of bread she'd saved from her meagre dinner, put the doll into the pocket and left the house.

When Vasilisa had walked a short distance, she pulled the doll out of her pocket, and, in a voice filled with sobs, she asked, "What will I do, little doll? I am terribly afraid that I will die a terrible death at the hands of the Baba Yaga. But at least if I die, I will be with my poor mother and father."

"Do not despair, child," replied the doll in a voice that sounded very calm and reassuring. "Your mother's blessings and her love will always be with you. Do not turn back. That would be worse than going to the home of the Baba Yaga."

Cold, tired and hungry, Vasilisa walked through the night. Just before dawn, she heard the thunderous noise of a horse galloping along the trail behind her. She crouched at the edge of the path and watched as a knight dressed in white rode a white stallion past her.

A few minutes later, she heard more hoofbeats and stepped to the edge of the path just as a man in red armour riding a red stallion passed her. Soon, the sun rose and drove the darkness of the night away. It wasn't very warm, but it did shine through the branches of the bare tree. She could see where she was going and began to walk rapidly.

Late in the afternoon, when the sun was low on the horizon, Vasilisa noticed a thin wisp of smoke rising above the trees ahead of her.

The Baba Yaga's house must be near, she thought.

It was almost dusk when she arrived at a clearing with a strange and very frightening-looking house in the middle of it. As she came closer, she discovered something that brought all her fear and terror back to her. The fence that surrounded the house was made of human bones and skulls.

She was about to turn and flee back along the trail when she heard the galloping of a horse. A knight in black armour rode by on a black stallion, and night fell. But it wasn't completely dark in the Baba Yaga's yard. An eerie light glowed from the eye sockets of each skull. Suddenly, a noise louder than a tornado came out of the forest. The ground began to shake. Vasilisa crouched in a shadowy part of the yard and watched as an old lady riding in a large mortar circled in the air and then landed beside the door of the house.

It was the Baba Yaga. Before she opened the door, the witch turned around and sniffed intently. "I smell Russian blood," she shrieked in a raw, rasping voice. Then she pointed to the spot where the terrified girl was trying to hide. "And I see a Russian girl. Do not try to escape. It is impossible. You must come into the house with me."

Vasilisa was so frightened that she could not move. So the witch walked over, grabbed her by the hand and dragged her into a very dirty house. "Why are you here?" she asked. "And be sure you tell the truth. I have a special punishment for people who lie to me."

"I . . . I . . ." Vasilisa stuttered, "I came for some of your fire." She told the witch about her stepmother and stepsisters, and how they'd sent her out into the night when all the fire had gone out.

When she heard Vasilisa's story, the witch cackled. "If you want me to give you fire, you'll have to earn it," she said. "You can start by warming up my dinner."

It didn't take long to build a hot fire. Vasilisa picked up the huge pot on the hearth. It was incredibly heavy, but she managed to swing it up onto the iron hook and push it over the flames. When the stew began to bubble, she ladled some into a huge bowl and took it to the table where the Baba Yaga sat, licking her lips in eager anticipation. The old woman quickly emptied the bowl. Vasilisa filled it again . . . and again . . . and again, until the pot was nearly empty.

"That's enough for me," the old lady finally said. "You eat the rest. Don't worry," she continued as Vasilisa hesitated. "I didn't use any humans to make this stew, just a pig, a side of beef, a few chickens, and onions, potatoes and carrots. No humans have come this way for a long time. I certainly miss them." And she eyed the girl hungrily.

As Vasilisa was filling her own bowl, she carefully picked

out a small chunk of meat and placed it in her pocket. She knew that her doll would be hungry too.

"Now, my dear," the witch said as she watched Vasilisa eat the stew, "I'll tell you what you are going to have to do tomorrow if you want me to give you some fire. First, you can give the house a thorough cleaning. Then you can wash the windows, inside and out, and after you've finished that, you can weed the front yard. And I noticed this morning that there isn't much chopped wood in the shed. You'd better get enough to last us for several days. It's going to be very cold at night.

"After you've finished those chores, get the large sack of grain from the storeroom. I want all of the chaff separated from the wheat. Then get dinner ready. I'll be home just after the black horseman rides by. If you don't finish all these chores, I certainly won't give you any fire."

Vasilisa quickly washed the two bowls and spoons and then spent over an hour scouring the enormous pot, which looked as if it hadn't been cleaned for months. The old lady sat in a rocking chair by the fire, watching the girl and puffing on a pipe filled with terrible-smelling tobacco.

When Vasilisa finished cleaning the pot, the witch pointed to a door in the corner. "You'll sleep in the closet. I'll be on the big bed right near the door. So don't try to escape."

Vasilisa left the kitchen, closed the door behind her, lay down, covered herself with a coarse, musty blanket and listened carefully. Soon, the Baba Yaga began to snore. Vasilisa waited some more. The snores continued. The girl pulled the doll out of her pocket, fed it the morsel of stew meat and whispered, "What can I do? I'll never be able to get all that work done, and even if I finish, it would be impossible to separate every grain of wheat from the chaff."

"Trust in your mother's love and her blessings," the doll replied. "All will be well."

Vasilisa dropped into a deep sleep, so deep that she didn't hear the snoring, which was getting so loud that the windows of the house started to rattle.

The next morning, the witch shook her awake. "Get up, you lazy girl," she snarled. "You have a lot to do today." Then she turned and walked out of the house.

The girl looked out the window. Just as the witch was climbing into her mortar to ride away, the man on the white horse galloped by and the grey light appeared in the east.

A few minutes later, she heard another horse. It was the red knight and his roan stallion. As the sun's rays fell across the yard, she gasped in amazement. The yard had been weeded and raked, and a stack of chopped wood stood by the shed door.

As the room became brighter, Vasilisa noticed that the windows sparkled. There wasn't a speck of dust anywhere. And, in the corner, there were two sacks. She opened one and found kernels of wheat. Before she opened the next, she knew what she'd find the discarded chaff.

Vasilisa gave a great sigh of relief. She had the whole day ahead of her with nothing to do but cook. She loved cooking. It was something she and her mother had done long ago. She sat at the table, looking out the window and thinking about what she might make for dinner. *I'll have to see what kind of supplies the old woman has*, she thought to herself.

First she headed to the vegetable garden behind the house. Weeds stuck up through cracks in the hard dirt, and chicken droppings were everywhere. *Nothing much could grow here,* she thought. *But I'm sure the Baba Yaga has vegetables. There were some in her stew last night. There must be a root cellar.*

There was. Vasilisa went inside and looked through the bins of unsorted vegetables. Many of the carrots, onions and potatoes she found had gone bad. But she found enough unspoiled ones for another stew.

She took the vegetables to the kitchen and then walked through the weeds toward a chicken coop she'd noticed at the back of the yard. The place looked like it had never been cleaned. Holding her nose, she leaned in and grabbed three chickens by the neck, took them over to a chopping block, picked up a rusty axe, beheaded the squawking fowl and then cleaned them.

Back in the kitchen, she looked in the cupboard for the spices she'd use in the stew she planned to make. The shelves were a mess. But after much searching, she found what she needed. When she had all the ingredients, Vasilisa began to prepare her stew. Within an hour, the room was filled with the delicious aroma of the evening's dinner.

The witch returned home just after the rider of the black stallion had galloped by and the sun had set. By the light of the glowing skulls and the moon, she could see the neat and tidy yard. She burst through the door, looked around the tidy kitchen and smelled the simmering stew. She seemed very surprised, but all she said was, "Get me my dinner, girl, and be quick about it."

The evening was pretty much the same as the first one. The witch ate nearly all of the stew, leaving only a little for Vasilisa, who saved some for the doll. While the girl was cleaning up, the Baba Yaga gave her instructions for the next day: clean the chicken coop, weed and spade the back garden, polish the bone fence, and then make dinner.

"Oh, yes," she said between puffs of her foul-smelling pipe, "I almost forgot. You'll find two large sacks in the shed. When they were being packed, some fool mixed up the peas and the lentils. I want you to separate them. You'd better get to bed right now," the old woman ordered. "You'll need all your strength tomorrow."

Vasilisa did as she was told. Then she fed the doll, who reminded her about her mother's love and blessing. That night she slept even more soundly than she had the night before.

When the Baba Yaga returned the next evening, she was amazed. She had given the young girl a list of tasks that no human being could complete in a day. But they were all done, and moreover, tonight's dinner smelled even more delicious than the previous night's.

After the witch had eaten, she spoke to Vasilisa. "Many things about my house must seem very strange to you. If you have any questions, you may ask them."

Vasilisa asked about the three horsemen. "That's simple," came the reply. "The knight on the white horse signals the coming of dawn. The one on the red horse is the rising of the sun, the one on the black horse, the coming of night. Do you have any other questions?"

"No," Vasilisa responded. "I was once told that too much curiosity can be dangerous."

"You are wise beyond your years," the witch said. "If you had been too inquisitive, I would have had to kill you and eat you. But now I have a question to ask you. I am amazed that you have been able to do everything I asked you to do. How is that possible?"

Vasilisa remembered her mother's warning about never telling anyone about the doll, and so she replied, "With my mother's love and her blessing."

Suddenly, the witch flew into a rage and shouted, "Mother! Love! Blessing! Those are words that I hate! They are about qualities of goodness that I cannot defeat. Get your shawl and leave. Never come into these woods again. Take one of those skulls on the gatepost. It will light your way home."

Vasilisa rushed through the yard, grabbed one of the glowing skulls and ran to the forest path. The skull sent a strong beam of light ahead of her, making the trail very easy to follow. By daybreak, Vasilisa was tired and hungry. She reached into her pocket and found a breadcrumb. She was tempted to pop it in her mouth. But she knew that if she didn't give the doll food, it would be unable to comfort and advise her. She fed the crumb to the doll.

When she asked what she should do, the doll replied, "You have already seen the power of your mother's love and blessing. Her power will continue to guide you. You must rest now."

It was nearly midnight on the second night when Vasilisa arrived at her house at the edge of the forest. She walked timidly toward the door, opened it and entered. The skull spread its light around the house. When the stepsisters saw her, they both began speaking.

"Where have you been?"

"What took you so long?"

"We've been freezing for days, and it's your fault!"

What they didn't say was that after Vasilisa had left the house, they hadn't been able to relight the candles or the fire.

"Put that lantern on the table where we can see it," the stepmother hissed, not noticing that the lantern was a human skull. Gradually, the light from the skull narrowed into a beam and pointed directly at the stepmother. "My eyes are burning," she shrieked. She got up and ran to hide in the corner, but the beam followed. The woman burst into flames and quickly turned into a pile of ashes. Then it turned on one of the sisters and chased her into another corner, and the same thing happened. The same happened to the other sister. Soon Vasilisa was alone, and the beam retreated into the skull.

Vasilisa swept up the piles of ashes, put them in the coal scuttle and lit a fire. Soon, she was sitting at the table spooning up a bowl of steaming oatmeal. She fed a little to the doll and then asked it, "What happened? Why did the light from the lantern turn on my stepsisters and my stepmother and not on me?"

"Perhaps," the doll replied, "the power of your mother's love and blessing was greater than the power of the Baba Yaga."

The next morning, Vasilisa buried the ashes and the skull lamp in the yard. By the time she had finished, the sun was shining brightly in a blue sky. Vasilisa went back inside the house, picked up the doll and put it in her pocket. Then she went outside and began to walk toward the village, ready to begin a new and happier life.

PROMETHEUS

AND THE GIFT OF FIRE

GREECE :: In Greek mythology, Prometheus, whose name means *forethought*, helped Zeus win the war that made him king of the gods. However, when Zeus turned into a tyrant, Prometheus opposed him. This story about how Prometheus created human beings and brought them the gift of fire was first written down 2,800 years ago.

From high on Mount Olympus, Zeus looked over the lands and seas he ruled. The forests and prairies that had been scorched during the great war had begun to turn green again. Rain clouds dotted the skies. Whitecaps scudded across the ocean's surface.

But something was missing. No animals grazed on the tall grasses or wandered among the trees searching for prey. No birds sang in the branches or soared high in the sky. No fish or dolphins leaped from the shining surface of the sea. Nor were there any humans. Like the other creatures, they had been destroyed during the battles that had made Zeus the lord of all creation.

Something must be done about this, Zeus thought. *The skies and lands and seas seem so empty without the birds and animals and fish that used to be there. I need someone to create animals and birds and fish and, most important, human beings. Who knows what interesting and enjoyable experiences I could have if once more there were creatures down there to visit?*

He decided to discuss the matter with Prometheus, the smartest and most creative individual Zeus had ever met. He had helped Zeus win the great battle. *If he helped me then, he might decide to overthrow me as well. If I give him something to do, he will be too busy to plot against me,* Zeus thought.

Prometheus listened intently as the lord of all creation explained what he wanted. Prometheus agreed to make creatures to fill the skies, lands and seas.

"Before you leave, send your brother Epimetheus to me," Zeus ordered. "I will give him gifts to bestow on your creations, gifts that will make their lives better."

While Zeus was giving Epimetheus instructions and providing him with the gifts, Prometheus descended from Mount Olympus and began the work of making all the creatures of the lands, seas and skies. He had finished most of his work when Epimetheus arrived.

"I am going to create human beings now, and that will take a great deal of time," Prometheus explained to his brother. "You can begin giving out the gifts to the animals, birds and fish that I have already made. And remember, think carefully before you give. You know that you have the habit of doing things first and thinking about the consequences later. That's why you get into so many difficult situations. Once you give something, you cannot take it back."

Epimetheus listened carefully. He promised his brother that he would think before he acted. Then he left to start distributing Zeus's gifts. He gave some of the animals sharp teeth and claws so that they could hunt. To others, he gave speed so that they could flee their enemies. To a few, he gave poison to defend themselves when other creatures attacked. Some of the birds received fierce talons so that they could dive from the air and seize their prey. Others got feathers of many colours so that they could hide in the flowers when they were in danger. To the fish, he gave gills so that they could breathe under water. To some fish, he also gave bright colours, like the birds, so that they could hide from the bigger, fiercer fish.

Epimetheus returned to his brother when he had finished. Prometheus stood back from the humans he had created, pride and love shining from his eyes. "Epimetheus, these are the most wonderful beings I have created. Look how they stand upright and how they gaze at the heavens, not down at the ground like the other animals. They are more wonderful than the people who were destroyed during the great war. I have made sure that they resemble the gods of Olympus. I love them and want them to have happy and full lives."

Prometheus bent close to the mud and clay figures he'd shaped and breathed on each of them. When he did, each creature came alive. They stretched their limbs and opened their eyes, looking at the world around them.

"Let me see what you have in your bundle of gifts," Prometheus said to his brother. "We must give them something that will make them greater than all the other beings I have created."

Epimetheus reached into his bag and began to rummage around. A look of alarm came into his face. Then he looked embarrassed. He said nothing, just hung his head, gazed at the ground and made little lines in the dust with his toes.

Prometheus waited for several minutes and said nothing. Epimetheus remained silent. Finally, the older brother spoke. "What's the matter, Epimetheus? What gift do you have for my wonderful human creatures?"

"N . . . n . . . nothing," came the stammered reply. "I wasn't paying attention when I gave out the gifts to the other animals. I wasn't thinking. Sometimes I gave an animal more than one gift. There are no gifts left."

At first, Prometheus wanted to rage at Epimetheus for his thoughtlessness and irresponsibility. But he knew that anger would not help anything. He sighed deeply and looked at his brother for a long time.

Then he said, "What will happen to these people? They don't have tough hides to protect them or fur to keep them warm. They haven't got sharp claws or great teeth to hunt and defend themselves. They cannot run fast or fly high or dive deep. They will have to spend their nights in fear. Without a gift, they are less than all of the other creatures."

For once in his life, Epimetheus thought as hard as he could, trying to find some solution to the great problem he had created. But he had no ideas.

Prometheus looked at his shivering, frightened human creations and shook his head sadly.

Epimetheus couldn't see Prometheus's brow furrowed in thought. Prometheus's eyes were focused on his creations, but he had turned inward. He was searching for an idea that could rescue his pathetic creatures.

At last, he stood up and exclaimed, "Fire! That is the answer! With the gift of fire, human beings will be able to do so much more than any of the other animals. They will be able to cook their food and keep warm at nights. They will be able to see after the sun sets, and the fire will frighten dangerous animals away. And there are so many other things. With fire, they can create metal tools and weapons the way Hephaestus does at his forge on Mount Olympus. With tools and implements, they can build homes and plow the fields. You didn't give fire to one of the other animals, did you, Epimetheus?"

"No," replied his brother, "there was no fire to give. You know that Zeus controls all the fire, and he doesn't want it to leave Mount Olympus. Your human beings will never have fire."

"That may be," said Prometheus. "But I will ask Zeus. Surely he is still grateful to me for helping him become the lord of all creation. Surely he will want these creatures who look so much like the gods to lead happy and full lives. He will be proud of them and pleased with himself for having made their existence so much better with the gift of fire."

Prometheus walked slowly along the winding uphill road that led to Mount Olympus. He knew that any meeting with Zeus would be difficult. The lord of all creation had a very suspicious mind and, even worse, a very bad temper. Very carefully, Prometheus planned what he would say and how he would say it. The well-being of the humans he had created depended on the success or failure of his meeting with Zeus.

He decided the best plan was to be straightforward.

Prometheus told the lord of all creation that he had created humans to be like the gods but lesser than the gods. He said that he had wanted Zeus to enjoy the company of human beings when he decided to travel from Mount Olympus. But because Epimetheus had given all of the gifts to the other animals, human beings had no way to live full and happy lives. Perhaps Zeus would consider another gift for them.

When he had made his proposal, Zeus responded, "And what would you suggest?"

"With a gift of some of the sacred fire from Mount Olympus," Prometheus replied, "human beings would not only be able to survive, they would be superior to all of the other creatures. They would be like the gods, and they would be good companions when the gods visited the lower world."

Prometheus could immediately see that his suggestion hadn't gone over well. Zeus frowned, his face turned red, and anger flashed from his eyes. "Never!" he roared. "Fire belongs to the gods. It will never leave Mount Olympus. Go back to your human beings and find your own way to help them."

What Zeus didn't say was that he was afraid that if the people ever got fire, they would become so powerful that they might be able to overthrow him.

Prometheus left Mount Olympus. That night, the rain began to fall. The wind blew fiercely. In darkness, the human beings huddled together and moaned softly in their misery. Some animals growled fiercely in the night. It was only because Prometheus was nearby that they didn't attack and devour the helpless people.

The next morning, he told Epimetheus about his visit with Zeus and described how miserable and frightened the human beings had been during the night. "I created them. They are my children, and I am responsible for them. I must find a way for them to become the noble beings I want them to be."

Prometheus gradually formed a plan. It was a very dangerous one, and if it failed, both he and the human beings would suffer greatly. He knew that even if it succeeded, Zeus would punish him terribly. But he also knew that he was responsible for the newly created human beings and that he must fulfill his duty, no matter what might happen to him.

At sunset, he gave Epimetheus instructions. "I want you to stay here and watch over the people until I get back. I'm going back to Mount Olympus to steal the sacred fire. Hephaestus does not tend his forge at night. The flames die down to gentle embers. I will bring an ember back and then teach the people how to use fire."

Epimetheus pleaded with his brother not to go. But Prometheus ignored him and started walking toward the top of Mount Olympus. This time he did not take the main road but travelled along an old, overgrown path.

As he walked, he felt that someone was near him. He turned, and in the very dim light he saw that he had a companion. It was Athena, the goddess of wisdom. She admired Prometheus for his ability to think everything through, and she always enjoyed the friendly discussions they had.

"Why are you walking here in the dark on this old trail, my friend?" she asked. He told her about his quest for the sacred fire and about the difficulties he faced in getting it without being noticed. "I don't know how to get an ember so small that it won't be noticed or how to get it to the human beings before it goes out," he said.

"Fennel," she quickly replied. "Take a long fennel stock and hollow out the centre of it. When you get to Hephaestus's forge, take a very small ember and put it into the hole you've made. The soft wood inside will catch fire, but it will burn very slowly and with a very small flame. It will be protected by the outside of the stalk, and no one will be able to see the fire when you take it back to your human beings. I will leave you now."

Prometheus followed Athena's instructions carefully, and stealing the fire was easy. By dawn, he was back with Epimetheus. He asked his brother to gather some dry branches. Then Prometheus placed the ember carefully in the middle of the tiniest dry sticks and blew gently on it. A small flame began to burn.

Soon, Prometheus had made a good-sized fire. "Come, my children," he called to the people. "Gather around the fire. It will make you warm." At first, they were frightened. But when a cold wind began to blow, they moved closer and held their hands toward the flames.

"This is fire," he said. "It will make a good friend or a bad enemy. If you learn to use it well, it will help you do many wonderful things. But if you are not careful with it, or you use it unwisely, it will be very destructive. You must listen carefully to what I teach you. The fire will help you become the most noble of the beings I have created."

As Prometheus taught the human beings, he waited for some kind of reaction from Zeus.

Zeus noticed smoke rising from the lands below Mount Olympus and sent his messenger Hermes to spy on Prometheus. When Hermes returned, he reported about the fire and how Prometheus was teaching the human beings. Zeus was furious, and although he didn't show it, he was also a little frightened. *Had Prometheus given the people the source of great power?* he wondered.

At first, he thought about flinging his thunderbolts from the sky and destroying all the people and maybe even Prometheus, too. But then he decided to wait. *It will be a greater punishment if I let the people get used to fire and all the wonderful things they can do with it,* he thought. *Then I could take it away. They would miss it terribly, and they'd be far more miserable than they were before. That would be the best revenge and punishment.*

Several weeks later, Zeus sent Hermes back to where Prometheus was teaching the people more wonderful things about fire. "Tell him he must give the fire back," Zeus instructed his messenger. "Tell him that if he refuses, I will punish his people terribly. Tell him that if I do, it will be his fault."

Prometheus listened as Hermes delivered his message, and then he replied. "Ask Zeus if he has forgotten that it is the law of Olympus that immortals can never take back what they have given. Tell Zeus that I cannot return the fire. It belongs to the people now."

When Hermes relayed Prometheus's message to Zeus, the lord of all creation knew that he could not carry out this plan for revenge and punishment.

"Bring Hephaestus to me!" he roared. His servants hurried to the forge, where they found the god of fire. He was working to create a new kind of metal that he said would be stronger than any other he had ever forged.

"Tell Zeus that I cannot come right now or my experiment will be ruined. Tell him I will come as soon as I can, with a gift of this new metal. He may find some uses for it."

When Zeus learned the reason for the blacksmith's delay,

he smiled. *This new metal Hephaestus is developing will fit nicely into my plans for Prometheus*, he thought.

Soon the blacksmith shuffled into the throne room and stood humbly before Zeus. The lord of all creation asked if this new metal could be used to make the strongest shackles and chains that had ever been forged.

"Yes," he said. "The prisoner you want to use them on must certainly be very powerful."

Zeus explained who they were for and how they were to be used. Hephaestus felt sorry, for he had always liked and admired Prometheus. But he quickly agreed to his ruler's demands, fearing that if he refused he, too, would be punished terribly.

It took Hephaestus many days to create the shackles and chains. He was a perfectionist, and he worked very slowly. Even though his new artifacts would be used to punish his friend, he still wanted to produce the best work.

Zeus could hardly contain his excitement when Hephaestus showed him the products of his labour. Then he summoned Kratos, whose name meant power, and Bia, whose name meant force.

"You must go to the place where Prometheus and Epimetheus live with the new people," he told them. "Then imprison Prometheus with these shackles and chains and take him to the steepest mountain in the Caucasus. Do not fear him; he will not resist you. He knows what will happen to him. He will accept his punishment as a condition for saving the human beings he created."

Bia and Kratos took the chains and began the trip down Mount Olympus. They were happy to please their master and even happier that their mission involved cruelty, for they enjoyed seeing others suffer.

Prometheus was waiting when they arrived. He did not try to escape. He knew that his punishment was the price he would have to pay for bringing fire to his people. When Bia and Kratos held out the shackles, he did not struggle. He allowed them to put the unbreakable clasps around his wrists and ankles.

As they led him away, each one holding two of the chains, Prometheus turned to his brother and the human beings. "Remember, Epimetheus, try to think before you do something. Be warned: do not take gifts from the gods. Tell my children to use the fire wisely and remember that it can be a good servant or a very bad master."

Prometheus followed behind Bia and Kratos like a meek dog. The road they travelled was long and difficult, across deserts, through wild forests and then up the steep sides of one of the Caucasus Mountains. The little group halted just below the snow line. On a sheer cliff, Bia and Kratos fastened Prometheus's chains tightly until their prisoner was splayed against the rock, his arms and legs stretched out.

"You will regret having angered Zeus. You can never escape," Bia said. Prometheus said nothing.

That night, bitterly cold winds lashed at Prometheus, tearing his robes away and leaving him naked to the elements. Morning brought no relief. After the sun rose, the worst part of his punishment began. A giant eagle flew close and examined this creature chained to the cliff. When Prometheus did not move, the eagle came closer and raked Prometheus's body with its sharp talons. It tore viciously at him, until it had created a ragged, bleeding opening. Then it thrust its beak into the opening and pierced his liver. Prometheus held his voice as long as he could, but finally the pain became so great that he shrieked in agony.

The eagle departed as the sun set. During the night, the fierce winds again howled around Prometheus and sent chills through his body. But when the daylight returned, Prometheus looked down to discover that his torn body had healed. It was as if the eagle had never attacked.

He was amazed and puzzled. Why had this happened? Had Zeus shown him some pity? He soon discovered the reason. The healing was really part of the punishment. The eagle returned that morning, and seeing what looked like a new victim chained to the rocks, it renewed its attack and clawed and tore at Prometheus's liver until the sun set.

This was to be Prometheus's life for eons—countless days of pain followed by bitterly cold nights of healing.

Zeus did offer Prometheus an escape from his torment, however. Every few years, Zeus's messenger Hermes would fly to the cliff, and in the early dawn, just before the eagle returned, he would hover in front of Prometheus and give him a chance to be free of his chains. "My master has instructed me to tell you that he will give you your liberty if," and here Hermes paused, "you will reveal to him a secret that only you with your ability to see into the future can know. If you will give him the name of the person who will attempt to overthrow and kill him, you can leave this cursed place and return to your brother and your human beings."

"No! Never!" Prometheus replied. "Zeus is a tyrant. He rules with cruelty and terror. I will not tell him what I know about the future. He must face his destiny, and he must accept the consequences that his evil ways will bring him."

Centuries of almost unbearable pain passed, but Prometheus, although he cried out in agony, did not complain about his punishment. He had served the people he created in the best way he knew. It was better that he should suffer for them than that they should live their lives in misery.

GLOSSARY

ANISHNABEG :: The name the Ojibway/Chippewa people of Ontario and Michigan use for themselves. The word means "the people."

ARAAR :: The name the Karuk people of northern California give themselves. The word means "the people."

BABA YAGA :: In Russian folklore, an old cannibal witch who frequently travels the countryside flying in a mortar (a bowl in which food or medicine is placed before grinding).

BAOBAB :: A tree found on the African savannahs. It can grow to over 20 metres in height. In addition to giving shade, it provides food, water and materials for making rope.

BILLABONG :: In Australia, a stagnant pool of water formed at the end of a dead-end channel of a river.

CARIBBERIE :: An Aboriginal Australian term for a ceremonial gathering.

CAUCASUS MOUNTAINS :: A mountain range located between the Black and Caspian Seas.

CHAFF :: The hard, dry outer coverings of grains and seeds.

CHAMELEON :: A lizard-like reptile that is noted for its ability to change its colour to that of its surroundings. It is also a skilled climber. The African chameleon can reach lengths of 45 centimetres.

COOLABAH :: A type of eucalyptus tree found near rivers in Australia.

EAGLEHAWK :: The largest bird of prey in Australia. It has a wingspan of up to three metres. It is also known as the wedge-tailed eagle.

EON :: A period of time that is so long that it seems immeasurable.

FENNEL :: A herb, the stalks of which are hollow and can grow to over two metres high.

GICHIGAMI :: An Anishnabeg name for Lake Superior.

GICHIMINISING :: An Anishnabeg name for Grand Island, located off the southern shore of Lake Superior.

HEDGEHOG CACTUS :: These cactus plants, from the desert regions of the American Southwest, grow fairly close to the ground and have very sharp spikes.

HOKI :: An edible fish found in the seas off New Zealand. It can swim to a depth of 1,000 metres.

IGUANA :: A lizard found in Central and South America. Adult iguanas can reach 1.5 metres in length.

ISHPABECCA :: An Ojibway name for the Pictured Rocks, which border the southern shore of Lake Superior.

KAREAREA :: A New Zealand falcon.

KIAKOMAKO :: A small tree native to New Zealand that grows up to 10 metres high. The Maori people of New Zealand used a sharp pointed stick from this tree as part of their fire-making equipment.

MAHOE :: A tropical, evergreen shrub. The Maori people used wood from this shrub to make fire. When rubbed vigorously with a sharp, pointed stick from the kiakomako tree, the wood catches fire.

MAHOGANY :: The African mahogany tree, which grows over 30 metres high, has grey-brown bark.

MESA :: The Spanish word for "table," used to refer to a flat-topped mountain.

MOUNT OLYMPUS :: Located in northern Greece, this mountain was believed to be the home of the Greek gods.

NIBULIN :: The word for *sweetheart* in the Wagiman dialect of Australia.

OPOSSUM :: A marsupial mammal the size of a cat, it is found in much of North America. It has grey fur and a hairless tail. When threatened, it lies on the ground as if it is dead.

PUEBLO :: The Spanish term for "village." The word was applied to the Native people of the Southwest who lived in villages.

RAKALI :: The official Australian term for "waterrat."

RANCHO :: A camp or settlement of small huts.

RAUKAWA :: The Maori name for Cook Strait, which runs between the North and South Islands of New Zealand.

REBOZO :: A large, rectangular piece of cloth often used as a shawl in Mexico.

SAVANNAH :: Grasslands that cover large areas of sub-Saharan Africa. Most savannahs have trees scattered across them.

SKOOKUM :: This word from the west coast Chinook dialect can have two opposite meanings. It can refer to something being good or positive, or it can refer to a frightening, powerful being who uses spirit powers for evil purposes.

SOOTY OWL :: A nocturnal bird found in eastern Australia. It gets its name from the dominant grey-black colour of its feathers and the black rings around its eyes.

TE IHORANGI :: The Maori name for the god of rain.

TE IKA-A-MAUI :: The Maori name for the North Island of New Zealand.

TE TAI-O-REHUA :: The Maori name for the Tasman Sea, located between Australia and New Zealand.

TE WAI POUNANAMU :: The Maori name for the South Island of New Zealand.

WAKA :: Outrigger canoes made by the Maori of New Zealand. Some were intended for one or two occupants. Others, reaching a length of nearly 40 metres, carried many men on long ocean voyages.

WIGWAM :: The main type of dwelling constructed by the Anishnabeg people of the Great Lakes region. Birchbark and woven mats were draped over a dome-shaped structure made of bent saplings.

THE TRAIL OF THE TALES

Each of the traditional tales retold in this collection has a long history extending back to a time when stories were passed on orally from place to place and from generation to generation. With each retelling, storytellers added, deleted or changed the emphasis of details. Many stories from lesser-known cultures became known to larger audiences after they had been collected by anthropologists.

Once stories appeared in print, they continued to change, particularly when they were retold for children. Retellings often reflected the tellers' own beliefs, values and attitudes about what kinds of stories were suitable for younger readers and listeners.

One of the most valuable resources for a person wishing to discover the wide range of fire-quest stories from around the world is Sir James George Frazer's *Myths of the Origin of Fire* (London: Macmillan, 1930). Frazer, who was one of the foremost students of folklore and mythology in the early decades of the 20th century, discovered hundreds of examples of fire-quest stories and presented brief summaries of them.

I have listed below the various sources I have consulted in retelling these traditional fire-quest tales from many lands.

HOW OPOSSUM BROUGHT FIRE BACK TO THE PEOPLE

I used the version found in Frazer's *Myths of the Origin of Fire* and supplemented his basic plot outline with research into opossums, the Cora people and the landscape in which they lived. Jan M. Mike has created a picture book version entitled *Opossum*

and the Great Firemaker: a Mexican Legend (Mahwah, NJ: Troll
Associates, 1993).

WHY THE SELFISH WATERRATS SHARE FIRE

I have drawn on several closely related versions of this
Australian story: W. Ramsay Smith, "The Discovery and Loss
of the Secret of Fire," *Myths and Legends of the Australian
Aboriginals* (London: George G. Harrap, 1930); Alan Marshall,
"How Fire Began," *People of the Dreamtime* (Melbourne:
F.W. Cheshire, 1952); and A.W. Reed, "Waterrat and Fire,"
Aboriginal Myths, Legends and Fables (Reed: Chatswood,
1993). An online version of Reed's retelling can be found at
www.nswfb.nsw.gov.au/page.php?id=651.

WHY THE PEOPLE RESPECT TORTOISE AND CHAMELEÓN

The source for this story is Melville J. and Frances S. Herskovitz's
Dahomean Narrative: a Cross-Cultural Analysis (Evanston:
Northwestern University Press, 1958). In addition to a wide-
ranging collection of tales from the Dahomey people of what
is now Benin in western Africa, the volume includes valuable
background information about the people and the cultural
significances of the stories they tell.

HOW COYOTE AND HIS FRIENDS CAUGHT FIRE

The use of a group of characters forming a kind of "relay" to
solve problems is a favourite motif in folktales around the world.
Many versions of this tale about members of a group that, after
one of them has stolen fire, take turns carrying the burning stick
back to their home, are found along the west coast of Canada
and the United States. In retelling this Karuk version, I have
drawn on "How Coyote Brought Fire: Spokane Tribe," www.
cometogetherarticles.yolasite.com/coyote-brought-fire.php; John
Vance Cheney, "How Squire Coyote Brought Fire to the Cahrocs,"
xtf.lib.virginia.edu/xtf/view?docId=modern_english/uvaGenText/
tei/CheCoyo.xml&chunk.id=d3&toc.id=&brand=default; "How

Coyote Brought Fire to the People: A Karok (Karuk) Legend, www.firstpeople.us/FP-Html-Legends/How_Coyote_Brought_Fire_To_The_People-Karok.html. John London and Sylvia Long have created an illustrated version of the tale: *Fire Race: A Karuk Coyote Tale* (San Francisco: Chronicle Books, 1993).

COYOTE CATCHES FIRE

Frank Cushing, an anthropologist who lived with the Zuni people for five years in the later 19th century, first wrote down this tale. It is published as "How the Coyote Danced with the Blackbirds" in *Zuni Folktales*, collected by Frank Hamilton Cushing (now available in a 1986 University of Arizona Press reprint). Gerald McDermott has published an excellent illustrated version of the story *Coyote: a Trickster Tale from the American Southwest* (San Diego: Harcourt Brace, 1994).

MAUI FINDS FIRE—TWICE

Although the Polynesian people from New Zealand to Hawaii tell several fairly similar stories about Maui, the versions are very different from each other, each one reflecting elements in the lives of the particular group. I have drawn on A.W. Reed's *Myths and Legends of Maoriland* (Wellington, NZ: A.H. and A.W. Reed, 1946); "Maui's Search for Fire," www.in-site.co.nz/miracle/links/objects/MAUISEARCHFORFIRET.pdf; "How Maui Brought Fire to the World," www.tki.org.nz/r/maori/nga_pakiwaitara/maui-mahuika/index_e.php; and "The Legend of Maui and Fire," whanaushow.co.nz/index.php/maui-and-fire. Peter Gossage has retold and illustrated the story in *How Maui Found the Secret of Fire* (Auckland, NZ: Penguin, 2009). In *A Book of Tricksters* (Victoria: Heritage House, 2010), I have retold a Hawaiian version of the story: "How Maui Found the Secret of Fire."

WHY MAPLES TURN A FIERY RED

I have drawn on nearly 40 years of reading tales about the Ojibway hero Nanabozho and spending summers and autumns in Michigan's Upper Peninsula, where part of this retelling takes place. The Nanabozho tales first gained wide attention in the middle of the 19th century when the New England poet Henry Wadsworth Longfellow wrote "Song of Hiawatha," which was loosely based on Henry Rowe Schoolcraft's *Algic Researches* (1839). Two extremely useful collections of Nanabozho tales are Emerson Coatsworth's *The Adventures of Nanabush* (Toronto: Doubleday, 1979) and Edward Benton-Benai's *The Mishomis Book: The Voice of the Ojibway* (St. Paul, MN: Red School House, 1988). "How Nanabozho Brought Fire to His People," a version of Nanabozho's quest for fire, can be found in Dorothy Reid's *Tales of Nanabozho* (Toronto: Oxford University Press, 1963). Elizabeth Cleaver's *The Fire Stealer* (Toronto: Oxford University Press, 1979) is a picture-book version of the story.

VASILISA AND THE BABA YAGA'S FIRE

Perhaps because it bears many similarities to the story of Cinderella, this narrative is one of the most frequently retold and adapted traditional Russian tales. I have drawn on *Vasilisa the Beautiful: Russian Fairy Tales*, edited by Irina Zheleznova (Moscow: Progress Publishers, 1966); "The Annotated Baba Yaga," www.surlalunefairytales.com/babayaga/index.html; and "Vasilisa," www.oldrussia.net/vas.html. Marianna Mayer and K.Y. Craft have teamed up to create an illustrated and somewhat different interpretation of the story in *Baba Yaga and Vasilisa the Brave* (New York: Morrow Junior Books, 1994).

PROMETHEUS AND THE GIFT OF FIRE

I first discovered the story of Prometheus while taking courses in English and classical literature over 50 years ago. Since then, I have encountered the myth in many adult and children's versions. In preparing this retelling, I have drawn from information in Barry B. Powell's *Classical Myth* (Englewood Cliffs, NJ: Prentice Hall, 1995) and "Prometheus: Greek Titan god of forethought, creator of mankind," www.theoi.com/Titan/TitanPrometheus.html. After over 40 years, *D'Aulaires' Book of Greek Myths,* by Ingri and Edgar Parin D'Aulaire (Garden City, NY: Doubleday, 1962) is still one of the best children's introductions to Greek myths. Leon Garfield and Edward Blishen have included the story of Prometheus in their *The God Beneath the Sea* (London: Longmans, 1970), a superb novelistic treatment of Greek mythology.

ACKNOWLEDGEMENTS

This collection of retellings of traditional stories about people's quests for fire would not have been possible without the help of many people. I am indebted to all those who have retold these stories over the centuries. From reading their adaptations, I have learned how different writers select and emphasize different details, capturing as well as is possible what the tales might have meant when they were told orally and adding their own interpretations, making the stories relevant to modern readers. To Vivian Sinclair of Heritage House, who encouraged me to undertake this project, and to Grenfell Featherstone, who offered wonderful editorial guidance, thank you. To Michelle Armstrong of Monsignor Fee Otterson Catholic School in Edmonton and her Grade 6 class, thank you for listening to early versions of the stories in this collection and for offering insightful (and mercifully charitable) feedback. Your responses have helped me make these retellings better than they would otherwise have been. My daughter, Dr. Clare Stott, a member of the third generation of teachers in our family, carefully read drafts of these stories and made important editorial contributions.

The dedication expresses my gratitude to two of the finest modern retellers of traditional tales.

Jon C. Stott, a retired English professor, taught children's literature at the University of Alberta for 35 years. He has been telling stories in schools since his children were in the first grade. He is the author of *A Book of Tricksters: Tales from Many Lands*, also published by Heritage House.

A writer, photographer and artist, Theo Dombrowski studied drawing and painting at the Banff School of Fine Arts and in the Fine Arts Department of the University of Victoria. Before retiring, he was a teacher in international education, primarily at Lester B. Pearson College of the Pacific near Victoria, BC. He lives near Nanaimo, BC.

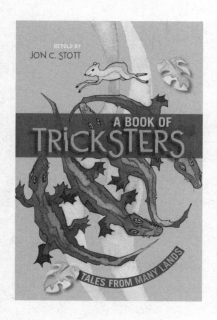

A Book of Tricksters
Tales from Many Lands

by Jon C. Stott

print: 978-1-926613-69-7, $12.95
epub: 978-1-926936-67-3, $9.99

For centuries, people around the world have been telling stories about tricksters—characters who solve problems by using their wits to fool others. Jon C. Stott has collected traditional trickster tales from 14 different countries, including "How Anansi Brought Stories to the People" (Ghana), "How Zhao Paid His Taxes" (China), "How Kancil Built a Crocodile Bridge" (Indonesia) and "How Maui Discovered the Secret of Fire" (Hawaii).

Books by Caroll Simpson

Inspired by their rich storytelling tradition, Caroll Simpson's engaging tales and vibrant illustrations encourage all young readers to further their knowledge of and respect for First Nations art, culture, history and mythology.

The First Beaver

print: 978-1-894974-50-9, $24.95
epub: 978-1-927051-23-8, $11.99

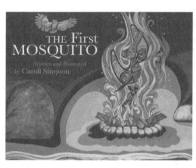

The First Mosquito

print: 978-1-926613-67-3, $24.95
epub: 978-1-927051-22-1, $11.99

The Salmon Twins

print: 978-1-927051-52-8, $24.95
epub: 978-1-927051-97-9, $11.99

The Challenger Family Library

With over 70 000 books sold, the Challenger Family Library is a bestselling series that illustrates the vaule of family, friendship and the lessons of nature. Inspired by Aesop's fables and the tales of the First Nations of the Northwest Coast, Jim Challenger's books are excellent resources for parents, teachers and anyone interested in the art of storytelling.

Eagle's Reflection
print: 978-1-895811-07-0, $9.95
epub: 978-1-926613-06-2, $8.99

Grizzly's Home
print: 978-1-894384-94-0, $9.95
epub: 978-1-926613-11-6, $8.99

Nature's Circle
print: 978-1-894384-77-3, $9.95
epub: 978-1-926613-18-5, $8.99

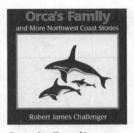

Orca's Family
print: 978-1-895811-39-1, $9.95
epub: 978-1-926613-21-5, $8.99

Raven's Call
print: 978-1-895811-91-9, $9.95
epub: 978-1-927051-06-1, $8.99

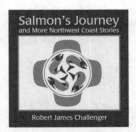

Salmon's Journey
print: 978-1-894384-34-6, $9.95
epub: 978-1-926613-23-9, $8.99